THE RETURN OF SANDRA LOVE

A NOVEL BASED ON TRUE EVENTS

STEVE PETERS

Published by Star Hill Publishing
345 Bahia Lane, Cape Carteret, North Carolina
28584

Available on-line at
www.theoutlawsandralove.com

©2015 Steve Peters
Contact at slppet@yahoo.com

Cover Art by Adam Thompson at
www.retrographics.biz

To all the folks who read the first book and told us they wanted more...God bless you all.

Acknowledgement

I'd like to express my gratitude to my friend and co-author Kay Stephens. When I first read Kay's original manuscript of The Outlaw Sandra Love, written, based on her tape recorded interviews with Sandra, I was intrigued by the storyline and Sandra's life. I started my own research and found that many people on the coast knew her and had some outrageous stories about her that they were willing to share, some true, others not. There was no doubt that she was an individual who's entire life was worth exploring. I traveled to Newport, Tennessee and met with the former FBI agent who had been her handler when she worked undercover there. My instincts were confirmed and my project became my passion. In the spring of 2013 we published the novel with great success, but we also received an overwhelming demand for more.

So she's back, and I hope all of you enjoy this story as much as I have enjoyed writing it. I'd like to thank all the people that have helped me with this story, but especially Tony Cummings from the State Bureau of Investigation and Myra Miller with the Carteret County Sheriff's office.

Be strong!

Steve

Table of Contents

Prologue

The two towering Carolina Pine trees stood seven feet apart and thirty feet behind the cabin. A 2'x4' had been nailed between them eight feet off the ground. Hunters call this a deer hang. They use it to hang a dead deer after a successful hunt. When a deer is taken in the field, it is normally gutted at the kill-site to reduce its weight, dragged to the hunter's vehicle with a rope that is tied around the animal's neck, and brought to the camp where it is strung up on the deer hang until the hunt is over and it is taken to a professional butcher for processing. What hung from this hang was an exception to the rule.

The lights from inside the cabin lit a small area behind it, but did not illuminate the deer hang that remained on the edge of the shadows in the dark woods. The sounds of the forest pierced the night, crickets chirping and the occasional hoot owl. The big man opened the back door and stepped out. He walked back toward the deer hang, he carried a backpack in his right hand and a bottle of beer in his left. He sat down on a blow-down log a few feet from the deer hang and looked up.

The half-moon cast some light through the pine trees and partly cloudy night sky. He lit a cigarette and watched the smoke waft up into the cool night air. Then he took another swig of beer. He appeared relaxed and eerily at home as he finished the cigarette crushing the butt out on the ground next to the mane of long blonde hair that hung down on to the ground from the young woman who hung from the deer hang.

The moonlight outlined the naked figure - the long white legs, her bare torso, and her naked breasts. Her young face reflected the horror of her condition; her panties had been stuffed in her mouth and several loops of duct tape wound around her head secured the gag. Her bulging, panic filled eyes followed his every move as rivulets of tears dribbled down her forehead. She hung from a rope tied around her bare ankles. The rope had been pulled over the 2'x4' and then tied off on a wall cleat that had been driven into one of the trees.

The man stood up and walked over to the cleat, untied the rope, and pulled down hard. The young woman's body rose two feet higher as her nostrils flared and she gasped out a muffled protest. She struggled to free her arms, tied behind her at the wrists and elbows. Her hair now whipped from side to side punctuating her effort to be free. He tied the rope off on the cleat. He reached down into the backpack and pulled a huge, gleaming-sharp knife out of the bag. He squatted beside her and held the knife in front of her face, her eyes transfixed on the blade as he ran his thumb gently up the sharp edge. She listened to his slow breathing and watched as the light, steamy vapor exited his emotionless mouth.

Prologue

Then, in a low guttural voice, he leaned in close to her face and whispered, "And now my dear, it is time..."

The Return of Sandra Love

The Croatan

The early morning sun glistened off the dew that covered the plants on the forest's floor. As the sun rose, the heat created an upward movement of air and the breeze gently swayed the light grasses that grew in The Croatan National Forest. As dark became light, the sounds of the forest could be distinctly heard; birds chirping, squirrels rustling in leaves as they foraged the forest floor for nuts, and the movement of other animals.

Shhh, the voice whispered in the ear of the young woman. "Don't move now."

The young girl froze in place. As she took a deep breath, a bead of perspiration appeared on her forehead.

"Wait..."

The girl squinted. She never spoke as her eyes stared straight forward.

"Now..."

KAPOW! The report of the rifle echoed in the quiet forest like an explosion.

The eight point buck dropped as if its legs had been pulled out from underneath it. Then it jumped up and ran from the trail it was on, back into the thicket of scrub trees from which it had emerged minutes earlier.

"Sandra! I missed him!" The young girl shouted in disappointment.

Shhh, the voice whispered. "Remember about being quiet in the forest," the woman sitting next to her spoke calmly as she let go of the binoculars that hung around her neck and gently put her hand on the young girl's back. "You got him."

"Really?"

Sandra Horne removed a pack of cigarettes and a Zippo lighter from her vest pocket and lit one, blowing the smoke up into the cool morning air.

"Sandra, can't he smell that?"

Sandra took another drag on the cigarette and blew the smoke up again above the log that the two hunters hid behind, it trailed off behind them.

"Sara, do you see the direction the smoke is going in?"

"Yes."

"We're downwind, that's why he didn't smell us at all."

"Can we go find him now?" Sara's face was strained with anxiousness.

"When I'm through this cigarette. You gut-shot him, hon, if we go after him now we'll be chasing him around the forest for miles. Let him lay down for awhile and bleed out, then we'll go find him.

In the meanwhile, I want you to eject the cartridge in your .30-30 and ease the hammer down into the safe position."

The fourteen year old, with thick, curly, sun-highlighted brown hair that hung down her back, responded and Sandra picked up the cartridge and handed it to the young hunter, "Put this in your pocket, you may want to keep it as a souvenir." As Sara put the spent round in her pocket, Sandra took another drag on her cigarette and asked, "Sara, is that your dad coming in behind me?"

Sara looked behind Sandra, "I don't see anyone."

"About a hundred yards behind me to your right."

The young girl peered out into the forest, "Oh, I see him. Yes, it's Daddy. How did you—"

"That's why your dad hired me, hon. Wait here, he'll walk in." Sandra finished her cigarette, field stripped it and put the butt in the pocket of her camouflage pants.

"I heard a shot, what happened?"

"I got him, Daddy. I got the eight point!" Sara shouted to her father.

Lane Brendel was a handsome, well-built, middle-age man. He carried a Remington 30.06 pump action rifle over his shoulder and a small backpack on his back. The former Marine, now a successful criminal attorney in Raleigh, hugged his daughter and looked over at Sandra giving her a thumbs-up.

"Congratulations, Sara. Where's the deer, Sandra?" He said in a low voice.

Sandra stood up and whispered, "You're going to have to work on that quiet thing, Sara."

"Sorry," the young hunter whispered.

"She knocked him down, but he got up and went back through the thickets. Let's give him another fifteen minutes, then we'll track him down. It's not 8:30 yet, is it?"

Lane looked at his watch, then shook his head marveling, "I have 8:25."

The three sat down on the log and Sara told her dad everything that had happened since they parked their Jeep on the fire trail off Star Hill Drive, walked back into the woods, and parted company more than two hours earlier. Her dad's chest seemed to get bigger and bigger with Sara's recounting of her adventure. The love between father and daughter was readily apparent. Finally, Sandra stood up, slung her strapped, 16 gauge double-barrel shot gun over her shoulder, barrel-down, and turned to her two clients. "Good to go?"

"Yes," Sara responded quietly.

Her father smiled.

"Sara, you follow me, Lane, you've got the rear. Follow my hand signals and no shooting. Roger?"

"Roger," the two responded in unison.

The threesome crept slowly into the thickets. There was a deer trail no wider than their shoulders that the animals had been using as cover when they moved from a small creek to a group of oak trees where they fed on acorns. Sandra had scouted this area all summer and for the first few weeks of fall. She had seen the dominant buck trailing behind the doe and knew that he used this path for it gave him cover all the way to the oaks. They exited the thickets and approached a small creek. Suddenly, Sandra stopped and stooped, her right hand went out from her hip.

SPLASH!

A small alligator slid into the creek and disappeared as it moved away from the hunters.

Sandra kept her hand in the stop position, stood up, and stepped down into the creek without making a sound. The water was shallow at this crossing point, yet she moved through it silently, like a ghost. Sara watched her and when Sandra waved her hand to follow, she tried to mimic her guide. The three tracked the deer blood for about a half mile. They crossed a field of tall grass slowly, as Sandra's keen eyes looked for signs. They reached another stretch of forest bordered on the right by a bog that the creek Sandra stopped and her two clients caught up.

"Do you think we may be pushing him?" Lane asked.

"No, he's down."

"How can you be so sure, Sandra?"

"Look behind you."

Lane and his daughter turned around, fifteen yards into the trees lay the buck.

"Sara, put your rifle on him and move in, if he moves shoot him again. Touch one of his eyes with the tip of your barrel, if he doesn't move, put your gun on safe and signal us to come over, understand?" Sandra instructed.

Lane stood behind his daughter smiling, he knew the buck was dead and Sandra was creating an adventure for his daughter, *I wonder where she learned to do that?* He thought.

Sara approached the deer cautiously, she touched it's head with her gun barrel, then she prodded the deer's head. She released the hammer to the safe position and turned around smiling from ear to ear. "We got him, Daddy!"

Lane walked over to his guide, "Thank you, I owe you one." He shook her hand. "Damn, Sandra, that's a good grip you have there."

The Croatan

"You're welcome, and I just might take you up on that some day. Do you want Sara to watch while I field dress it?"

"Yes, but let's ask her."

They walked over to the young hunter who was running her hands over the deer's horns.

"Daddy, that's a nice rack isn't it?"

"Yes it is, Sara. Now, do you want to watch Sandra field dress the deer?"

"Yes, but can you take my picture first?"

"You bet!"

Lane pulled a small camera out of his backpack and took a couple of pictures with Sara and the deer, then with Sandra, Sara and the deer. Sandra returned the favor with Lane and his daughter and eventually Sara took a few pictures of Lane and Sandra.

Sandra laid the deer on its back and Lane held it by the antlers. Sandra removed her ex-husband's Ka-Bar from the sheath on her left hip and made an incision from the sternum to the crotch, the deer opened up. "There's a lot of blood in here, because of the gut-shot. Come closer, Sara, I want you to smell this."

Sara moved a bit closer tentatively, Whew! She wrinkled her nose. "That stinks."

"Well, if you've done this enough, you get use to the smell, but it's not perfume is it?"

"No way!"

Sandra took off her camouflage jacket and rolled her sleeves up. She placed her arms inside the body cavity up to her elbows. She cut the windpipe and throat and then the membranes that held the guts to the spine. Suddenly, all the deer's innards rolled out as Lane tipped the deer to one side away from his daughter. Finally, she cut off the deer's scent glands on the hind legs explaining to Sara what they were and how deer use them, especially when they're in rut.

Sandra sheathed her knife, "Lane, if you can tie your tow rope around his head; I'm going to go over to that bog and wash up. See if you can find a branch big enough so we can both drag, be sure you get his front hoofs up alongside his head, don't want to break that rack. I'll just be a minute."

"Yes sir!" He smiled as he saluted Sandra.

She waved her hand at him as she turned and walked up over the hill and down to the bog.

"She's pretty good isn't she, Daddy?"

"Yep, she's something special."

"She reminds me of Mom."

Lane was silent.

Sandra walked down the hill to the edge of the bog. She bent down and washed the blood off her hands and arms. The sun was starting to warm the November morning. She looked up and a black vulture was flying across the bog, almost directly toward her. She watched the bird as it glided to her left and landed in a tree not twenty feet from where she stood. Her view was blocked by a few trees between her and the bird, but she could see that another vulture was in the tree, pecking on some carrion. She couldn't see the carcass, but she knew that it was very unusual for two vultures to be sharing a carrion off the ground. She moved around the trees that stood between her and the birds and up the hill to get a better view. Slowly, the two vultures came into view.

"Daddy, can we come down here again next year I really like Sandra..." Sara's voice trailed off as her eyes widened. Lane turned around. Sandra was walking down the hill, in a daze. Her big green eyes were welled up with tears. She looked as if she was in shock.

Lane reached out and grabbed her, "Sandra?"

Sandra didn't speak. She put her arms around Lane, she was shaking. Lane held her for a few moments, as he looked at his daughter's concerned face. He grabbed Sandra's shoulders and held her at arm's length, "Sandra, you're scaring Sara. What the hell's wrong?"

Sandra reached up and wiped her eyes. "Over there..." She pointed up the hill.

Sara started walking up the hill. Sandra saw her and broke away from Lane. She ran after Sara and grabbed her from behind. Sandra's green eyes narrowed and she brusquely told the teen, "Sara, you are to stay here with the deer. Do I have your word?"

Sara's face reflected Sandra's sternness, "Y-yes."

"Everything is going to be alright. Your dad and I are just going to walk to the top of the hill. We'll be back in a few minutes, I promise."

"Sandra, what's going on?" Lane asked again.

Sandra bent over and picked up her shotgun, "Sorry, guess I lost it there for a minute. Lane, come with me."

"Tell me what's going on."

"You'll see for yourself in a minute. Sara will be just fine, I promise."

The two walked to the top of the hill. Sandra pointed down toward the bog.

"Jesus!" Lane gasped.

At the bottom of the hill the body of a naked, young woman hung crucified between two trees. Her long blonde hair hung down from her head, her chin rested on her chest and her body was

covered with blood. Her ankles were tied
together and the two vultures were perched on
her shoulders, feeding.

The Return of Sandra Love

The Body in the Forest

"Sara, when we get in the Jeep please sit in the back seat, I want to talk to Sandra," Lane spoke quietly to his daughter.

Sara watched her father as he pulled the clip from his rifle and removed his orange hunting cap. He just didn't seem right.

"Are you okay, Daddy?"

Like any father would, Lane kept thinking, *That was someone's daughter*. He looked at his daughter, "Come here." He reached out with both arms and hugged Sara tight as if he was protecting her from every evil in the world. Then he kissed her on the forehead.

Lane took Sara's rifle and ejected the five remaining shells.

"Pick those up for me, honey, thanks."

"Yes, Daddy." Sara's curiosity had grown as the three of them had not spoken a word on their hike back to the Jeep, but she could tell this was not the time to question her father. She noticed that her dad had that thickened white saliva you get on your lips when your mouth is dry. She took her canteen off the side of her hip and handed it to her father.

The Return of Sandra Love

"Thanks," he sat down on the tailgate and gulped the water down as Sara picked up the bullets and put them in her cartridge box. Then he handed her back the canteen. "See if Sandra needs some."

She walked around to the front of the Jeep, Sandra leaned against the right front bumper smoking a cigarette.

"Water?"

Sandra stared out at the forest, lost in thought.

"Sandra?"

Sandra turned toward the young girl, "Oh...yes, thanks." She took the canteen and sipped some of the water, then she handed it back and took another drag on the cigarette.

"What happened out there, Sandra?"

"You have to ask your dad, hon," Sandra nodded to her right. Lane stepped up beside his daughter.

"Sara, there was a dead body in the woods and it was not something I wanted you to see."

"Oh..."

"Lane, if you're ready, we need to get to a phone and call the sheriff's office."

"Sure, hop in the front, Sandra. Is there somewhere close we can call from?"

"Yes. I have a friend in Cape Carteret, she's a magistrate there. I think Sara will be able to stay with her for awhile, rather than go back to the hotel alone."

"Good, I couldn't leave her alone, not now."

******

Claire-Anne Bolt was a petite woman with a pixy haircut and an assertive personality. She was well known and well liked in the small town of Cape Carteret and was active in local politics. Her husband worked at Camp Lejeune. She had a daughter, Karen, who was twelve. At 4'11" Claire-Anne was four inches shorter than Sandra. They were both forty years old and they were friends. They had met the previous year, in the summer of 1979, when there had been an episode between Sandra and her ex-husband, a Marine who had been injured during a deployment. Domestic violence is always a sad thing. Love and hate, some say those two walk hand in hand. Sandra, however, was capable of holding her own and both she and her husband were arrested and charged. Eventually, they both dropped the charges, but the damage was done. Her husband received a full disability discharge from the Corps and moved home to Charlotte where his parents lived. He filed for divorce in January of 1980 and it had been finalized just a few months ago.

"Hey, Sandra! Looks like you've been hunting, any luck?"

"Hey yourself girlfriend. We have a problem," Sandra, Lane and Sara walked into Claire-Anne's office. "Claire-Anne, this is Lane Brendel and this is his daughter, Sara."

"You the trial-lawyer, Lane Brendel, from Raleigh?" Claire-Anne asked.

"Yes," he responded.

"Well, we've all heard of you, Mr. Brendel."

"Claire-Anne, we were out in the Croatan this morning. There's a body in the forest and we need to call the sheriff's office right now."

Claire-Anne's face went stern, "Hunting accident eh, did any of you shoot him?"

"This is no hunting accident Claire-Anne, she wasn't shot. This is a homicide and we've got a weirdo out there somewhere. You follow?" Sandra emphasized her question.

"Yes."

"We'll have to go out there and show them where the body is; can Sara stay with you until we return?"

"Sure." Claire-Anne turned toward Lane, "If you need, she can spend the night with my daughter and me. Just let me know."

"Thank you, Claire-Anne, if at all possible we'll pick her up. Can I have a number just in case?"

He turned toward Sara. "You okay with that, Sara?"

"Yes. Do you think we can get the buck?"

"I'll try my best, hon," Lane replied.

Claire-Anne picked up her desk phone, "I'll call Bob now."

******

"Sheriff Bob, line one, it's Claire-Anne Bolt and she says it's urgent."

"Urgent eh, I'll take it here, thanks, Myra."

Sheriff Bob Baker moved away from the two deputies standing in the middle of the squad room and picked up a desk phone pressing down on the blinking line button.

"Claire-Anne, Bob, how can I help you?" The sheriff listened, *Hmmm...hmmm...*what? He gasped out.

The two deputies turned around.

"Yea...yea...okay, we'll be there in twenty minutes." He hung up and spun around. "Bill, Tony, let's go. We have a body in the Croatan!"

*****

"Sweet Jesus!" The sheriff stared at the body hanging in the trees. The two deputies that were with him turned away in disgust. It took them a couple of minutes to recover their composure. The three men, Sandra, and Lane stood there staring at the horror before anyone spoke.

Sheriff Baker broke the silence. "Bill, you need to hustle back to the car. I want every available deputy out here now. Get on the phone and call SBI, I want as much help as they can provide. Tell them what's out here. We need an investigation team to secure this site. They'll probably be here overnight, so tell them to come prepared. We'll need the medical examiner and make sure we have enough four-wheel drive vehicles for everyone. Bill, get this right the first time, we don't have much of a signal out here and it will start getting dark in a few hours."

"Okay, boss."

The deputy started to walk away.

"Sheriff Baker, this is federally owned land, should you contact the Forest Service or the FBI?" Sandra asked.

"You said your name was Sandra Horne?"

"Yes."

"Thank you Miss Horne. Guess I'm not quite myself right now. Feds too, Bill."

"Do you have any idea who she is, sheriff?" Lane asked.

"No." He turned toward the deputy that was hiking back to their vehicle, "Bill, have them bring a list of any females reported missing in the last few months." He turned back toward Lane, "And your name again, sir?"

"Lane Brendel, I'm an attorney. My practice is in Raleigh."

"Yes, I've heard of you." The sheriff took out a notebook and started writing. "You two were out here hunting together?"

"Yes, with my daughter. I hired Sandra as our guide."

"Where's your daughter now?"

"We dropped her off at Claire-Anne's after we found the body," Sandra responded.

"Did she see any of this?"

"No." Sandra and Lane responded together.

"Good, we'll keep it that way. Which one of you got that buck?"

"My daughter harvested it. It was her first take."

"Let me know where you're staying and I'll be sure the buck gets to you. He's a great deer for a first take."

"The Quality Inn on Rte 58 in Peletier."

"Okay. Nothing more to do now than wait."
Baker sighed as he took a few steps up the hill
away from the body. He was a hunter and had
been in the forest many times. The November
afternoon was sunny and the temperature had
risen to the mid-sixties. The forest was beautiful,
as he looked around everything seemed normal,
until he turned back and looked again at the
body hanging in the trees. "What kind of asshole
brings a woman out here to do that to her?" He
commented angrily as he pointed at the body.
"And cuts her eyes out...what kind of sick pervert
does that?"

The body was cutup badly, blood covered both
sides of her torso and legs.

"Sheriff, if you don't mind," Sandra turned toward
the body and pointed, "he didn't kill her out here.
He tortured her and killed her somewhere else."

"How do you know that?"

"There's no blood running down her arms from
her palms where he drove in the nails, she was
dead when he hung her up. Look on the ground,
there's very little blood, if he did this here, there
would be blood all around. Those are ligature
marks on her wrists and elbows, he tied her
arms behind her back before he cut her up. And
I'd bet that she was hung by her ankles when he
did it, there's a disproportionate lack of blood on
her feet compared to the cuts on her body. I'm
sure you noticed the rope around her ankles has
some excess line hanging from the knot, that's

where he cut her down. Yea, she was upside down when he did this. Oh, and I'd be looking for a big strong man, there's no drag marks on the body, he carried her in here and she's hung pretty high, he's tall alright."

"What the hell...what are you, Sherlock Holmes?" Baker asked.

"No, but I am a fan. Oh, and I'd bet the birds took her eyes."

"She's also the best tracker I've seen in years," Lane commented, "any idea which way he came in and left Sandra?"

"Well, the closest fire trail in from here is on the other side of the bog, up that hill. If it was me, I'd have walked in the edge of the bog, no tracks. If you want, we can take a hike around the bog and see if we can pick up his trail. I don't think she's been out here more than a day or two."

"Tony, stay here. We're going to take a hike. Don't go near the body, or let anyone else, until I return. Anything happens or anyone shows, put one in the sky."

"Got it, boss," the deputy replied.

"Have either one of you gone near the body or touched it?"

"No," Lane responded to the question as Sandra shook her head negatively.

Sandra led the two men slowly around the edge of the bog. As she got to the other side she stopped. Her head turned from the bog to the hill and back to the bog, then back to the hill. Nothing. She took a few more steps and then crouched down on her haunches. She looked again at the terrain.

"He came out here," Sandra pointed at some bent grass by the edge of the bog. She stood up and started walking up the hill, Lane and the sheriff in tow. About thirty yards up the hill she stopped and then waved the two men forward.

"There."

The two men looked at the ground, a couple of leaves were splattered with blood. Sandra turned around and looked across the bog. The body hung prominently between the two trees.

"He stood here and picked his spot," she pointed across the bog, "maybe early Sunday morning."

"Damn Sandra, you are something else," Lane said as he turned and looked across the bog.

"That's pretty impressive, Miss Horne," the sheriff agreed.

"My friends call me Sandra," she stuck out her hand.

"Bob, Bob Baker. Somehow, I think we're going to be friends too."

Sandra smiled and shook his hand, then she took her orange hunting cap off, shook out her thick reddish-brown shoulder length hair and gently placed her hat over the bloody leaves. "Let's see if we can find where he parked his vehicle, maybe we can get you some tire prints." Sandra started up the hill.

Both men watched for a moment as Sandra's natural wiggle caught their attention. Sheriff Baker looked at Lane and blew some air out of his mouth as he shook out his hand. Then the two of them followed Sandra up the hill.

Twenty minutes later, the three stepped onto the sandy fire trail that came in from Rte 24. Sandra looked at the ground and walked up the trail a few yards, she pointed at the ground.

"These are his."

"Are you sure, Sandra?" The sheriff asked. "This is hunting season, these could have been made by—"

"Pretty sure. Look at these footprints between the tire tracks. See how much deeper they are than the others, he was carrying her."

In the distance behind them they heard a gunshot.

"Okay, seems we've got company. Let's head back," the sheriff turned and pulled his pistol from his holster. He fired a shot up into the air.

The macabre scene lay out across the bog as the three of them walked down the hill and around the bog. The contrast between the beauty of the forest and the horror of the crime scene made everything seem surreal to Sandra as they approached the men.

"Mac, good to see you again," the sheriff extended his hand, "sorry about the conditions, looks like we have a real freak on our hands."

Mac Farmer was a rugged looking man in his early forties with a Kirk Douglas, Spartacus haircut. He had worked for the State Bureau of Investigation for ten years, he was currently assigned to the Jacksonville office. He was dressed in slacks, a mock turtle neck and a corduroy sports coat. He wore a shoulder holster that carried his .357 S&W Magnum revolver and a pair of low-rise LL Bean hiking boots that had been well broken in; they matched his belt and the leather on his holster.

"It appears that way. Derrick Strong is coming up from the Wilmington Office, he'll take charge since it's federal land. Bill said he should be here in about an hour. Who are your friends?"

"Mac, this is Sandra Horne and Lane Brendel, they found the body."

"Good to meet you," he nodded at the two who stood behind the sheriff. "Are you the attorney from Raleigh?"

"Yes," Lane acknowledged.

"Have either of you touched the body?"

"No, Sandra replied, "we tried to stay as far away as possible, but there were a couple of vultures on her when we first got here."

"About what time was that?"

"Around 9:30," Lane answered.

"How do you know?"

Lane raised his left hand; he was wearing his old USMC watch with a camouflage wrist band.

The SBI Agent smiled, "Marine too?"

"Yep."

"Oorah! Did you take the buck I saw on the way in?"

"No, my daughter did."

"Did she see this?"

"No. Sandra made sure she didn't."

The sheriff stepped in, "Mac, the three of them were out here early, Lane's daughter is at Claire-Anne's, but she's not a witness. Sandra has a theory about this, I think you should listen to her. She's also a hell of a tracker. She's found how he came in and left."

"Okay, why don't you show me what you've got? Can we get some tape up and secure the scene,

I don't want anyone through the tape until the feds and the guys from the crime lab get here. Not even the medical examiner. Bob, you know how important that is, right?"

"I've got four deputies out here now, I'll take care of it."

"Sheriff Bob, you might want to get someone out on Rte 24, so no one drives in on that fire trail until they have a chance to take casts of the tire tracks and footprints," Sandra suggested.

Mac Farmer raised his eyebrows.

"Thanks, Sandra, I'll do that right now." The sheriff smiled and walked over to his deputies, they huddled up.

"Why don't you show me what you've got, Ms Horne?"

"Why don't you call me Sandra."

"Okay, Sandra, I'm Mac."

Sandra, Lane and Farmer walked over to the body and Sandra explained why she thought the homicide had been committed elsewhere and how it was done. Farmer nodded and asked Sandra to show him the path on the other side of the bog. The two took the agent around the bog and up the hill to the fire trail pointing out the blood drops, under Sandra's hat, on the way. Farmer looked and listened as Sandra pointed out the tire tracks and footprints, some deeper than others. She shared her thoughts on the man's size and strength.

On the way back he asked, "Do you have any training or background in law enforcement, Sandra?"

"I have some friends in law enforcement, but I haven't seen them in years. I had a close friend that taught me tracking years ago, but every forest is different. I've been hunting the Croatan for three years now, guess I just love the beauty and serenity it provides."

"Where are you from?"

"Well, originally I'm from the mid-west, but my ex-husband was a Marine and I guess you both know what that means. I've lived in Peletier for the last three years." Sandra's half truth seemed to satisfy the agent. When they returned to the scene an FBI agent was onsite. The medical examiner and an investigator from the state crime lab were also present.

"Special Agent Derrick Strong!" Farmer announced as the threesome arrived. "They sent us the best."

A tall black man dressed in an expensive suit stood just outside the tape that the deputies had run from tree to tree about thirty yards up the hill from the body. When he heard his name he turned around.

"Mac Farmer, how have you been?"

"Good, all good, until this." They shook hands.

"You've been hiking?" Strong looked at Sandra and Lane.

"Derrick, this is Sandra Horne and Lane Brendel, they found the body and a lot more."

"So I heard from Sheriff Baker," he extended his hand to shake hands with Sandra.

"Easy Sandra, this is the feds," Lane stage-whispered.

The two shook hands. Strong stood a foot taller than Sandra, but as he shook her hand he could feel the diminutive woman's strength.

Strong extended his hand to Lane, "The attorney from Raleigh?"

Sandra's head turned, her face a bit puzzled.

"Yes," he turned toward Sandra, "I get that a lot."

"Nice to meet you, I've followed some of your cases," Strong remarked.

Lane nodded.

"I'd like to get statements from you two, how long are you going to be in town?"

"I was planning to go back Wednesday night."

"Mac, can we use your office tomorrow?"

Mi casa es su casa, mi amigo. Farmer looked at Sandra and Lane, "How about we let these folks go, it's getting pretty late and I want to take you and the investigator from the lab over to the trail so we can get those tracks cast. Sandra, Lane, here's my card, why don't you call me around 9am tomorrow and we'll set something up." While Farmer was talking, Derrick Strong looked over at the body again. "Derrick, you FBI guys can afford cards now, right?" Farmer casually tapped Strong on the shoulder, it seemed to jar him back from thought. He reached inside his suit jacket and pulled a small leather folder out and handed each of them a card.

"Thanks for your help, talk to you tomorrow. Come on Mac, time to go to work."

As the two agents stooped under the yellow tape and gathered the others together, Lane and Sandra started to walk back to his Jeep. Sheriff Baker passed them headed toward the group inside the yellow tape.

"Thanks for your help folks, one of my men took the buck back to your Jeep," the sheriff informed Lane as he hustled toward the group.

"Sheriff Bob, if you can, will you retrieve my hat and give it to one of the agents? It's my lucky hat," Sandra asked.

"Will do."

******

The Return of Sandra Love

"That was a day," Lane turned to Sandra as he drove onto Star Hill Drive heading toward Claire-Anne's to pick up Sara, "you sure know how to give your clients their money's worth."

Sandra laughed nervously, the comment triggered memories of her past, "Always a good thing."

"Listen, this has been a day, I don't know about you, but I'm hungry. Would you like to have dinner with Sara and me?"

"That's kind of you, Lane, I'd love to, but I'll take a rain check tonight. You and Sara enjoy your evening together, I've got family to feed."

"You've got kids?"

"Well, I think of them that way. I have two dogs, Zack and Cooper and a cat, Jerry. How about tomorrow night?"

"That's a date. You pick the place, nice please."

They picked up Sara and then dropped Sandra off at the Piggly Wiggly parking lot, on the corner of Rte 24 and Rte 58, where they had met at 5am that morning.

"Sandra, thank you very much for helping me get my buck. I had a lot of fun, I hope we can do it again next year." Sara hugged Sandra as they got out of the Jeep.

"You are very welcome, Sara."

"How about we meet here at nine tomorrow morning, we can grab some coffee and then call the SBI office." Lane suggested.

"Sure, see you then." Sandra got into her gray-green, 1976 Ford 150 pickup and drove back to her trailer in Peletier. The day's events ran through her mind over and over again. She prayed for the young woman in the forest. She turned left on Peletier Loop Road and then turned onto the dirt road that went back to the path that led to her lot in the forest.

"Hey guys!" Sandra was greeted at the door by her two Walker Hounds, Zack and Cooper. She slid her Ka-Bar off her belt and set her shotgun down in a corner. "Who's hungry?" Lots of tail wagging. "Good evening Jerry." Her black, green-eyed cat, Jerry Crosby Miller, was curled up on the recliner he considered his when Sandra was not sitting there.

Zack and Coop were less than a year old. Sandra had rescued them from the shelter where she volunteered. They were half-brothers, same dad, but different moms. Zack was a month older than Coop. The dogs had been brought to the shelter with five other Walker puppies when an elderly gentleman in Morehead City, who was a breeder, died. Sandra and Jerry had picked out the two and brought them home about six months ago. Both were white with black markings and tan trim. Zack had a blanket pattern on his back while Coop's was a saddle pattern. She let them out to pee. As the dogs did their duty, Sandra refilled their two water bowls and then called them back into the trailer.

"Sit!" Sandra extended her hand out over the dog's heads.

The two dogs sat obediently in the kitchen as their mom filled their two food bowls and placed them on the floor a safe distance from each other. Coop was a food-whore. He was less assertive than his older brother, who he tended to follow in the field, but dinner was a different story and Zack knew he had to keep his distance. Jerry jumped up on the counter. Sandra picked him up and he began to purr. She stroked him for a few minutes and gave him some kisses. Then she put him back on the counter.

She pulled some leftover chicken-noodle-corn soup out of the fridge, poured it into a pot and put it on the stove as she took some crusty bread out of the bread-box, heated the oven and warmed the bread while she set the table.

"How's tuna sound, Jerry?" Sandra opened a cabinet and took out a can of tuna, put it in Jerry's bowl and placed the bowl on the kitchen table. She put some ice in a glass and filled it with sweet tea. Then she pulled the bread out of the oven, poured the soup into a bowl, took her camouflage jacket off and sat down at the table. Jerry jumped up on the table.

"So how was your day?" Sandra asked as she buttered her bread. Jerry looked up, licked his lips and kept eating. "Oh, mine? I guess you could say it was a little weird. Yep, that's it, a little weird."

After dinner she cleaned up and stepped outside, walked over to two tree stumps that she and her ex-husband had cut when they first moved to the lot and lit a cigarette as she sat down. Sandra looked up at the blanket of stars and the half moon. She enjoyed the clear night sky the coastal area offered. Sandra smoked her cigarette, it helped her unwind. She had been dry for over three years now. As she sat on the stump and peered out into the darkness, she remembered the nights she used to spend with her friend Billy Arrowood on the front porch of his cabin in Tennessee. He had taught her many things about living in the forest. She remembered him telling her about the rhythm of the woods. Each forest has its own rhythm. The sounds of birds like owls, nocturnal animals like deer or possum, insects like crickets, the croaking of tree frogs and the wind and weather, they all tell the story of what mother nature has in store for that night. When you live long enough in the forest, as Billy had, the rhythm is familiar to you. Slowly, Sandra became aware that the forest's rhythm was off tonight. It was silent.

May have a bear that's wandered in, she thought as her head cocked a bit and her big green eyes scanned the darkness. She took a sip of the sweet tea she had brought with her. It was cool for a late November night, the temperature was going to drop into the low forties.

Hope those officers dressed warm. Sandra finished the cigarette and tea. She rubbed her bare arms, it was cooling down and she was just wearing her camouflage T-shirt and pants. She stood up, stretched her arms out arching her back and yawned, "Bed time."

She went back into the trailer, hit the lights and went to bed. Zach and Coop joined her in bed.

Nice body, the big man behind a tree up the path thought, *I may have to come back sometime. Might be an interesting experience changing your mind about helping the cops.*

Back Stories

Sandra pulled into the strip mall parking lot. Lane's Jeep was there parked next to a black 1979 Mercedes-Benz S-class sedan. She pulled up in front of the two vehicles and got out. Lane, Sara and a woman in her middle sixties got out of the Mercedes.

"Hi, Sandra!" Sara came running over to Sandra and gave her a big hug. She turned around as the two adults approached, "This is my nana."

"Sandra, this is Sara's nana and my mother-in-law, Jenny Hughes. Jenny, this is Sandra Horne, she has taken very good care of us while we were on our adventure."

"It's nice to meet you, Miss Jenny."

The older woman's stern face seemed to relax as Sandra acknowledged her respect with her greeting. "A pleasure meeting you, Ms Horne. Thank you for taking such good care of *my* Sara and Lane."

Message received, Sandra thought. "It was my pleasure, she's a very special young woman. You are very fortunate."

Jenny Hughes was silent.

"Jenny, thanks for coming down on such short notice. I'll see you tomorrow night at the house. And I will see you in my dreams, sugar." Lane lifted his daughter and gave her a big hug.

"Thanks, Daddy, I had fun."

"How about we use my car, Sandra, not a lot of room in that cab of yours."

"Sure." Sandra started walking toward the Jeep.

"Uh...this one Sandra," Lane pointed at the Mercedes.

"Oh, I thought that was your car," Sandra turned toward the older woman and smiled.

"Well, Christmas is next month, I'll ask Santa to bring me one," Jenny looked at Lane then back at Sandra, "nice meeting you."

"Good-bye, Sara."

"Good-bye, Sandra."

The two got into the Mercedes. "Where are we going, Sandra?"

"Over to the island, there is a great breakfast place in Emerald Isle called Mike's. Perfect for jeans and casual. They have a pay phone we can use."

"If I didn't get a chance to tell you, you look very nice this morning."

"Thanks Lane, Cleaned up a bit this morning. Wore my good jeans for you."

"Do you like to shop?"

"Sure."

"Open the glove compartment, there's an envelope inside for you."

Sandra opened up the box and reached inside. She pulled out an envelope with her name on it, she opened it. There were six one hundred dollar bills inside.

"Thanks Lane, but this was my fee for three days, we only hunted for one and most of that day was a nightmare," Sandra took two hundred dollars and put the rest back in the glove compartment.

"Okay, let's use the rest to go shopping when we're through with the interviews."

"Lane, do you like me?"

"From the moment we met."

"I take it you're rich and somewhat famous. When I was young I spent a great deal of time with rich, powerful people, *ad nauseam*. Money doesn't impress me. Even in a small coastal area like this, there are a few men I've met that think because they have money, it entitles them to be treated better than others or treat others worse than they wish. I value honesty, loyalty and integrity. My philosophy is pretty simple, treat others like you want to be treated, be respectful, be polite, be responsible and when I screw it up please don't tell me I'm going to burn in hell, cause you don't really know. Oh...turn here."

"Here?"

"Yes."

"Guess we're not going shopping?" Lane asked.

"I can't. I have a big date tonight and I have to get ready for it," Sandra turned and smiled at Lane. Then she reached over and patted him gently on his thigh.

"A date eh. Where are you going on this date?"

"Captain Charlie's in Swansboro, best seafood on the coast."

Lane continued the charade, "And what time is your date?"

"I'm meeting him there at 8pm."

"Have you dated this guy before, do you like him?"

"From the moment I met him."

Lane smiled.

The two got out of the car and went into the diner. Lane called the SBI office in Jacksonville.

They wanted to see the two of them at 11am.
They ordered breakfast and then Lane started,
"Why don't you tell me a little about yourself?"

"Gentlemen first please."

"Okay. I was born and raised in Raleigh. My dad
was a lawyer and my mom taught elementary
school. I'm an only child. Loved sports, but by
high school I was concentrating on football and
track. Attended NC State on a football
scholarship and wanted to go into law
enforcement when I graduated, FBI. The bureau
requires three years of related experience post
graduation before they'll consider you. They
have several fast-tracks, accounting,
law, foreign language, but most recruits are just
in the chase the bad guys track. I had an offer
through one of my dad's friends to go with the
state police, but I was told my first job would be
3am in the morning looking for drunks on the
inter-states. It didn't have much appeal. A friend
of my dad's was with the bureau and my dad
and I had lunch with him. He had gone another
route after college, the Marine Corps. Sounded
exciting to me and always good on a resume. So
I signed up and went up to Quantico for OCS.
Four hundred and twenty started the program,
two hundred of us were commissioned, I was
ranked twelfth in our class. Spent four years in
the Corps, made Captain before I got out in
November of '62. The FBI academy recruits in
the summer for their classes that start in
October, it corresponds with the federal fiscal

year. Rather than wait a year to apply, I started law school at Duke, I loved it."

"Why didn't you just go to law school after college?"

"Wild oats, I don't know, guess the Corps had some adventure appeal. Have you ever had an adventure, Sandra?"

"No, with the exception of the last twenty five years."

Lane laughed.

"How did you meet your wife?"

Lane paused, "Sandra, my wife passed two years ago, ovarian cancer at thirty-eight."

"Lane, I am so sorry."

Lane went quiet for a moment and Sandra just let it hang as she sipped her coffee. Then the waitress brought breakfast.

After she served and left, "Lane, I lost my mother to liver cancer two years ago."

"Really?"

"Seriously, been there, done that. Very painful."

"Annie was the love of my life, Sandra. I will love her forever. So, what's your story?"

"Well, I've been married twice. The first time I was eighteen, too young. My husband was a lady's man and the marriage didn't last two years. I have one son, from that marriage, he is a senior in college in Illinois. I have a Bachelor's in Business Administration from Valparaiso University. After I graduated, I worked three years for the FBI and then went into banking. I worked in banking for four years before I met my second husband in 1976, he was a Gunnery Sergeant in the Marine Corps. We got married in 1977 and I moved here because he was stationed at Camp Lejeune. He was injured during a deployment exercise in 1978, he received a full disability discharge last year, but he started drinking and the relationship went south. He moved out and filed for divorce in January, it was just finalized this summer. Lane, I've known some great men in my life, but I haven't been lucky with love. The greatest accomplishment in my life is my son, Tony. He is my pride and joy."

"So I take it from your degree and your background in banking, you were in the accounting track with the bureau?"

Sandra paused for a moment, "I think it would be fair to say I was on the business side," Sandra smiled. "How's your breakfast?"

The two finished breakfast and drove to the SBI office in Jacksonville. They met with Derrick Strong who asked them to tell their story while he recorded them. There was not much they could add to what they had previously told the sheriff and Mac Farmer. Farmer gave Sandra her lucky hat back. They had no additional information on the victim. After finishing their written statements, they left and as they were coming back through Swansboro, Sandra pointed to Captain Charlie's.

"That's where I'm going to have dinner tonight."

"*Hmmm*, well, hope you hit it off with this guy."

******

Lane Brendel walked into Captain Charlie's restaurant at 7:50pm. The smell of sea food filled the air.

"Nice."

The restaurant was warmly lit with wall sconces and indirect lighting. In the lobby a hostess stood behind a small wooden podium that held a reading lamp. There were two dining rooms, one on either side of the lobby. The room on the right had fewer tables, but it did have a bar.

"Can I help you, sir?" The hostess asked.

"Yes, I'm suppose to meet someone here for dinner. I'm probably a little early."

"Would you like to wait in the bar?"

"Sure."

"Who are you waiting for?"

"Her name is Sandra. I don't know if she made a reservation."

"You won't need one on a Tuesday night off-season. The bar is over here," she escorted Lane into the bar, "I'll bring her in when she arrives."

There were two couples having dinner at separate tables and three men at another table smoking cigars over coffee. One woman sat at the far end of the bar. She wore a black cocktail dress that exposed her well toned legs from the thigh down to the expensive leather heels she wore. She had long black hair that hung down to the middle of her back. There was a tumbler in front of her on the bar and an expensive looking clutch bag next to the glass. Lane sat down two stools over as the bartender approached.

"Good evening, sir, what will it be tonight?"

"Chivas Regal on the rocks, thanks."

Lane looked at his Rolex a couple of times as he sipped his scotch, 8pm came and went. As he waited for Sandra, he glanced into the mirror behind the bar. He watched the woman each time she lifted her drink. Her long neck stretched up as she raised the tumbler to her full red lips that matched her well manicured nails, she swallowed the last of her drink. The woman opened up her clutch bag and removed a gold Cartier single flame butane lighter. She lit her cigarette as the bartender approached Lane. *Now there's a class act,* Lane thought.

"How are we doing here, sir, can I get you another?"

Lane looked at his watch, 8:20pm. "Yes, looks like I've been stood up," he replied.

"Very good, sir." The bartender turned to make the drink.

"Well, that makes two of us," the woman commented softly as she looked at Lane in the mirror.

Lane turned toward the woman and took a good look at her beauty as he responded, "These things happen, who were you waiting for?"

"Some big-shot attorney from Raleigh, I met yesterday."

Lane took a double-take, "Sandra?"

The woman turned and faced him, "Good evening, Lane, you're late."

"Wow!" Lane stared at his date. "I-I didn't recognize you." Lane slipped off his stool and walked over beside Sandra. "You are gorgeous!"

"Can I get you another, Sandra?" The bartender asked as he put Lane's drink on the bar.

"I'm good, Eddie, I think we'll eat now that my date's arrived. Thanks for the help, you and

Betsy were great," Sandra's response alerted Lane to the depth of the conspired deception he had just experienced.

Lane, reached in his pocket and pulled out a money clip. He dropped a twenty on the bar, "I think I may be out of my league tonight. Keep the change."

"She made us do it," Eddie smiled.

"I understand completely."

"I didn't see your truck outside, did you park down the street?"

Sandra grabbed a black shawl that hung from the back of the bar stool, "No, came in a cab."

Lane escorted Sandra to a table, pulled out her chair, and when she was seated, sat down across from her. He stared at her as she looked at the menu. The candle on the table flickered light off of Sandra's cleavage. He had never met anyone so intriguing. In the indirect lighting of the room and the candle light on the table, Sandra looked twenty five. She had smitten him with her beauty, but there was an earthiness about her, a sexuality, that he had not seen before. He liked it, and her flirtatious sense of humor. Sandra looked up from the menu and caught him staring as the waitress approached.

"I'm Ashley, I'll be your server tonight, are you ready to order?"

The Return of Sandra Love

"I can recommend the flounder, it's grilled and covered with sautéed crab meat, delicious, but not too filling. Ashley, I'll have a side salad with Italian dressing on the side and no other sides please."

"Sounds good, make that two, and a couple of glasses of your Mouton Cadet white," Lane followed.

"Just one glass please, Ashley, I'll just have water tonight."

"Good to go," Lane folded his menu, took Sandra's and handed them to the waitress.

As the waitress left, Sandra turned to Lane, "Guess you should know, I'm an alcoholic."

Lane leaned forward, "How long dry?"

"Over three years now."

"Guess the drink at the bar was..."

"Club Soda and a lime."

"Good for you, excuse me a moment."

Lane walked over to the bar, gave his drink to the bartender and canceled his wine order. As he returned to the table Sandra spoke, "You didn't have to do that, but thanks. You are a very charming man, Lane."

"And you are a most intriguing woman, Sandra. Do you think it is fortuitous, our meeting at this point in our lives?"

"When you say this point, you're referring to our availability?" Sandra asked.

"Yes."

"Availability and vulnerability. Do you sometimes feel vulnerable?"

"Yes, but not because of money or success, it's my heart. I just don't know if I'm ready; then there's Sara and Jenny."

"You feel alone?"

"Yes."

"So do I."

"What do you do about that, Sandra?"

"I've started my new family with Zack and Coop, the two Walker Hounds I got this year and I have my cat Jerry, we've been together for almost ten years. I have many friends here on the coast. I'm not exactly a loner personality, but I enjoy the time I spend in the forest, it offers both beauty and solace as well as the challenges it provides. Lane, don't get me wrong, I miss the human touch, but as I've told you I don't feel lucky about love."

"Maybe you're just one of those women who can't pull a good man out of a Cracker-Jack box?"

"Maybe."

"Sandra, I've known you for two days, I've never met anyone like you before, are you some sort of enchantress?"

"Yes."

"No really, I'm serious."

"I'm being serious with you Lane. If you expect to have a relationship with me, we have to be honest with each other. That's the basis of all relationships, trust. I got your back and you've got mine. I was once what you might think of as an enchantress. I cast my spell on you when you came into the bar. I gave you a glimpse of how I used to make my living, *enchanting* for the Chicago Outfit. Do you understand what I'm saying?"

"I'm not sure."

"When I was twenty one, I was a call girl for the mob in Chicago."

Lane sat silently. Sandra sipped her water, bracing herself. Lane stared at her for a few moments, a frown slowly appeared on his face, then he pulled his chair out as if he was going to leave. Instead he leaned forward, "You've been carrying that baggage around with you for some time, haven't you?"

Sandra was surprised at his empathetic response, she had not expected it; her eyes moistened, "Yes."

"Not anymore. That ends tonight, Sandra, no more baggage. I don't care what you were, I only care who you are."

"Oh, Lane..."

"Okay, here we are," Ashley brought the tray of food to the table and put the plates down in front of them.

"Excuse me." Sandra bolted up from the table and rushed to the ladies room. She looked at herself in the mirror. *What's happening to me? Who is this guy? Get a hold of yourself, this is just a fantasy.* She grabbed a paper towel and wet it in the sink, she dabbed her eyes and looked in the mirror, Lane was standing behind her.

"I've got your back."

Sandra held the damp towel in front of her, her hands shaking. He walked over to her, took the towel and dropped it on the counter behind her and cupped her face in his hands. He leaned forward and kissed her gently on the lips. "You okay?"

She grabbed his head and kissed him with all
the passion and pain she had been carrying for
the last few years. He wrapped his arms around
her and kissed her back. Her head spun. He
pulled back and dropped down to where her
neck met her shoulder, his mouth opened and
he gently kissed her neck. Sandra went limp as
her breathing quickened.

"Oops! Sorry." An older woman who was having
dinner with her husband stood behind them.

Lane let go and spun around, "N-not at all, I
think we're finished in here. Ready, hon?" He
wrapped his arm around Sandra and escorted
her back to the table. She sat down and he
pushed in her seat, then he sat and looked
across at her. She was still breathing deeply, her
head was down and she was picking at her food.
Again he asked, "You okay?"

Sandra dabbed her eyes with her napkin and
slowly raised her head, her big cat-green eyes
stared into his, "What the hell are we doing?"

"Whatever makes you happy. It's been a long
time since I made a woman happy."

******

Lane opened the door to his hotel room and
waited as Sandra walked past him. Once in the
room Sandra turned, "Is this right?"

He walked over to her and put his hands on her
upper arms, "Let's talk later." He bent over and

kissed her on the cheek, then her neck and shoulders. The tingling went through her whole body. Sandra's breathing became faster as she felt her body growing warmer and warmer. She also felt strange, as a hundred things flew through her mind at once. It occurred to her that she and her ex-husband had never spent a night in a hotel room, she hadn't been in a hotel room with a man in more than eight years. She felt weak, she was not in control, then she felt Lane's hands unzip the back of her dress, it slipped to the floor and he stepped back to look at her as she stood there in her heels, black silk panties and bra. She smiled at the handsome dark haired man standing in front of her.

"You are exquisite," he told her. He reached out and turned her around. He unfastened her bra and slipped it down over her shoulders. He drank in the muscular form of the woman in front of him. Sandra's body was in the best shape of her life, well toned from her lifestyle. He turned her around and Sandra's large chest caught his eyes. She reached up and put her arms around his neck.

"Now," she whispered.

Lane swept her up in his arms, Sandra kicked her heels off and they dropped to the floor. He laid her on the bed and she pulled down the bedspread as he removed his clothes, all of his clothes. Sandra grinned, Lane's body was beautiful and he was ready for her. She relaxed her head exposing her neck, parted her lips, and took a slow deep breath. Lane lay on top of her and kissed her open mouth with his tongue as his right hand roamed over her breasts, belly and thighs. He slid down her belly and slowly removed her panties. Sandra's breathing grew rapid and erratic as he pleasured her with his mouth. He watched as her belly rose and tensed and then fell only to rise again and again until she climaxed.

"Enough," Sandra gasped as she motioned him to come up.

Lane lay down on her again, as she pulled her knees up. He kissed her neck, squeezed her breast gently and entered her. Sandra moaned softly as she arched her back, then Lane brought her to a second climax, Sandra smiled, satisfied. A few minutes later Lane climaxed as Sandra wrapped her legs around his back. As he lay on top of her, Sandra kissed his neck and rubbed his muscular back and butt.

"That was nice," Sandra whispered, "I think you may have killed the albatross."

"You were wonderful, Sandra. I think I needed that as much as you."

The two lay in bed and talked late into the evening, more details and feelings. They drifted off to sleep in each other's arms.

******

Lane came out of the hotel lobby, Sandra stood next to the Mercedes smoking a cigarette.

He put his suit case and suit bag into the trunk. He was dressed in jeans, a flannel shirt and a light jacket. "When can I see you again?" Lane asked as they got in the car and headed to Sandra's.

"Whenever you want. Turn right here, then left on the second dirt road."

Lane followed her direction.

"Stop here, this is my lot."

"Where's your home?"

"Just down that path a bit."

"Can I see it?"

"Sure, if you have the time?"

"I have to go back this afternoon, but I have my hiking boots on."

"I'll change out of this dress when we get to my trailer. I can fix you some breakfast and introduce you to my family."

"Zack, Coop and Jerry, I remembered."

The two walked down the path, they came to a small ridge where Sandra's trailer came into view. She stopped.

"Nice." Lane remarked as he took in the beauty of the forest, "It's quiet back here."

Shhh, Sandra whispered, "Something is wrong."

Vengeance is Mine

Sandra took off her heels and ran down the hill, across the bridge and up to her trailer.

"No...no...no...AIEEEEEE..." Sandra's scream filled the forest as Lane raced up behind her. She was kneeling on the ground looking into the woods next to the trailer. Zack and Cooper hung by their necks from a Red Oak tree branch, their throats had been slit and they had been disemboweled.

"Son of a bitch!" Lane shouted as he saw the two dead dogs.

Sandra wailed as she knelt on the ground and held her head with both her hands. Lane stood behind her for a few minutes while she emoted her sorrow. He reached down to help her up, but she threw her hands up into the air, looked at the sky, and screamed, "Why? Why? Why can't I have a little happiness? Just one day, just one fucking day, if I'm that evil why don't you just burn me in hell?"

Sandra collapsed on the ground and cried. Lane stooped over and picked her up in his arms, she wrapped her arms around his neck and continued her sobbing.

"He doesn't work that way, Sandra." Lane stroked her black wig and held her as he would his own daughter. After a few minutes passed, he lowered her to the ground.

"Sandra," he held her by the shoulders as her big, green, tear-filled eyes looked up at him, "where's your cat?" Lane asked.

"Jerry!" Sandra pushed away and ran to the front door of her trailer.

"Sandra, nooo..." Lane shouted as he ran after her.

Sandra opened the door to her trailer and out jumped Jerry Crosby Miller.

Sandra bent over and picked him up, "Hello baby," she blubbered.

Jerry started to purr.

"Come on," Lane took Sandra's arm, "we're going to call Farmer right now!" He took her back to the car and they drove over to Piner's Store and phoned Mac Farmer. Less than an hour later, Mac Farmer and Derrick Strong were at the trailer with an investigator from the crime lab.

"Sandra?" Farmer asked as he looked at the woman in the cocktail dress with long dark hair.

Sandra looked up, but didn't speak.

"You guys have a real freak on your hands here," Lane was clearly upset as he spoke to the

Vengeance is Mine

two agents, "Sandra thinks this is his way of telling her not to interfere in his business again."

"After Monday in the woods, we all knew what we had on our hands, Mr. Brendel, but this, this is just about as sick as I've seen," Strong responded," why don't you see if she's up for a walk through the trailer."

Lane walked over to Sandra, she was sitting on her stump. She had held Jerry in her arms for the past hour.

"Listen, they want you to walk them through the trailer, see if anything is missing or out of place. Are you strong enough for that?"

Sandra stood up slowly, "Yes," her voice was softer, but filled with resolve. It was different than that of the high spirited woman he had just spent the better part of two days with.

"I know you're feeling down, but this is important. They want to find this bastard as much as you do."

"No, Lane, not right now they don't."

Strong, Farmer and a young man with glasses walked over to the two.

"Sandra, this is Brent Wilkes from the state crime lab, if you're ready we'd like to do a walkthrough in the trailer," Farmer pointed at the sandy haired young man.

"We didn't have a chance to meet Monday in the forest, sorry for your loss," Wilkes commented.

Sandra remained silent.

"Miss Horne, I've dusted the handle and the front door for prints, would you put these on before we go inside?" Sandra handed Jerry to Lane. She put on a pair of Latex gloves the investigator gave her, as she did, Brent spoke. "I'll take the lead with Miss Horne, even though you're gloved, please don't touch anything." The two agents nodded.

Wilkes stepped up into the open entrance to the trailer, Sandra followed. She stepped into the living room and then right and into the kitchen. She looked around, there was no blood. She walked over to the counter and then back into the living room.

"He killed them outside," her voice trembled, "dust the cookie jar on the counter. I keep their *bone-nummies* in there." Sandra's voice went higher as she referred to the coined word she used for the dogs' treats. She wiped her tears away and fought off the pain. "It's been moved. There's no blood in here. He let them out and then lured them back to him with the treats. He was here Monday night late. I had a feeling, but brushed it off. That won't happen again." Her voice sounded stronger.

The three men stood in the living room as Sandra walked to the far side of the room and flipped the hall light on. She looked down the short hallway toward her bedroom at the end of the hall and the bathroom on the right, nothing. She walked down the hall as the men followed.

"What's in here Sandra?" Derrick referred to a door in the hall on the right just off the living room.

Sandra looked back, "Water heater and some storage. You can dust it, he may have been curious too." Sandra stepped into the bathroom and looked around, nothing. She stepped out of the bathroom and turned facing the men, "My head is starting to clear. If he rummaged around in the trailer, he probably wore gloves. This guy is crazy, not stupid."

Wilkes pressed his lips tightly together in affirmation.

Sandra stepped into her bedroom and turned on the overhead light. To her left, on the front wall of the trailer, was a man's chest-on-chest dresser. Several pictures of her son Tony were in frames on top. A full-sized bed with a patch-quilted bedspread and four pillows stood, unmade. A small night stand and lamp were in the far corner. She looked around, then walked past the foot of the bed and opened up a double door closet on her right. She reached up and pulled the string. A single bulb light came on. She looked at her wardrobe. Half the closet had jeans, hunting pants and shirts on hangers. On the floor were several pairs of boots and sneakers. The other half was full of expensive clothes and dress shoes that were neatly arranged in a rack on the floor. A shelf ran the full length of the closet. Half filled with caps and gloves, the other side with expensive leather purses and hats. Wilkes watched from the doorway.

"I don't see anything here."

"Where do you keep your underwear?" He asked.

She walked back over to the chest-on-chest and opened one of the drawers. The drawer contained underwear and lingerie. Sandra looked at it, counting in her mind.

"It looks fine."

"Do you mind?" Wilkes asked as he waved his hand around the room.

"Go ahead," Sandra responded with an edge of finality.

Wilkes dropped down on his knees and looked under the bed.

"Any monsters?" Sandra asked trying to relieve some of the tension.

Wilkes flashed a small flashlight under the bed, then he reached under and his gloved hand came out holding something small and fuzzy. He stood up, "Hairball."

"Jerry!" Sandra smiled as she envisioned her cat hiding under the bed.

Wilkes walked around the bed and opened the drawer to the nightstand. Inside were two handguns, a Beretta .25 semi-automatic and a Colt M1911 .45. In between the two guns was a small vibrator. Wilkes closed the drawer and walked over to Sandra.

"Miss Horne, We'll need a couple of hours here."

"Sandra, please." She responded.

"Okay, and I'm Brent. Sandra, we'll need a couple of hours here inside and out. Do you want to grab a cup of coffee and come back a bit later?"

"Thanks, can you give me a few minutes to change?"

"Sure." Brent grabbed the edge of the door with his thumb and finger and pulled on the door. It closed to the jam as he joined the other two in the hall.

Sandra took a deep breath and then unzipped her dress and let it slide to the floor. She stepped out of her heels, picked up the dress and dropped it into a small clothing basket beside the dresser. She turned toward the closet and froze. She turned around and grabbed the dress out of the basket.

The Return of Sandra Love

"Mac, will you ask her about the dogs, I could take care of them for her," Brent offered as he talked to the two agents in the living room."

"I'll ask—"

"Brent!" Sandra shouted from the bedroom.

The three moved quickly to the bedroom. They opened the door and Sandra was crouched on the floor in her bra and panties.

"He took what I wore in the forest."

"What?"

Sandra stood up as the men stared at her. She tore the wig off her head and ran her hand through her thick auburn hair.

"My camouflage T-shirt, panties and hunting pants are missing. I was wearing them Monday night when I went outside."

"Okay, Sandra," Brent murmured, taken back by the semi-nude woman two feet in front of him, "why don't you get dressed and we'll talk outside."

Sandra changed out of what she wore and put on fresh underwear, a pair of jeans, brown calf-high boots and a tan cotton V-neck top. She slipped on a brown leather coat and put the wig away. Before she and Lane left, she walked over to her two dogs, "I will find you in heaven, my babies."

Lane led her away.

******

"So, they're going to take care of Zack and Coop?"

"Brent said he would. I'll make some crosses when I get back." Sandra lit a cigarette and then sipped her coffee. "I could use a drink right now," she muttered as she looked out the window of the diner at the gray day outside.

"Sandra, this is a tough thing to have dropped on you like this. What are you doing tomorrow?"

"Making crosses."

"I meant for Thanksgiving."

"Oh, I didn't even remember. Tomorrow is Thanksgiving? I usually help out at the soup kitchen in Morehead City."

"I need a favor. Please don't say no. Come home with me today, spend Thanksgiving with Sara, Jenny and me. If you don't, I'll worry sick about you. It'll just ruin Thanksgiving," Lane smiled.

"Geez, Lane, how good company do you think I'll be?"

"I think you're looking at this wrong. Try, how good company do you think we'll be? I don't think being with my family will hurt. Sara adores you, and so will Jenny, after I speak with her.

You know I have feelings for you. Sandra, say yes."

"Can I bring Jerry?"

"Sure."

Sandra's smile was faint, "Yes."

When they returned to the trailer, Sandra went inside and packed a suitcase. The agents were outside finishing up. She came out of the trailer with her suitcase and Jerry, in his cat cage. She turned and locked her front door. Before they left Sandra walked out to where the dogs had hung, Brent had placed them in a body bag.

"Here," Sandra pointed at some impressions on the ground, "and here, those are his too. See the small space at the top of the print, exactly the same as the ones in the forest."

"Thanks, Sandra, we'll get him," Brent tried to reassure her.

"Take care, Sandra, try and enjoy the day tomorrow. This could have been much worse. We'll get this bastard," Mac promised.

"I'm going to ask for some additional resources on this, we'll be in touch. Sorry for your loss," Derrick Strong consoled.

Lane gave them his business card and wrote his home number on the back. He told them Sandra was going to be staying for the holiday. If they needed anything, just call. He grabbed her suitcase as she picked up the cage and the two walked her trail back to the car. On the way up to Raleigh, Sandra said a silent prayer for her boys. Then she made a vow.

The Return of Sandra Love

Inside the Beltline

Lane Brendel's home was on St Mary's Street off Glenwood Ave in Raleigh. The home was old and stately and the area designated historic. Lane turned into the driveway that led to a freestanding three-car garage at the rear of the home and a planted island circle in the front; he pulled up in front of the double-door main entrance.

Sandra looked at the huge home, "This is your home, Lane? I've been in museums that weren't this big."

"I thought you weren't impressed by money."

"I'll need to buy a bigger trailer after this." Sandra looked at the house and plantings as she got out of the car. Lane popped the trunk.

"I just want you to enjoy your stay."

"I will. You have been very kind, I won't forget."

"Sandra!" Sara came out of the house, jumped off the pillared porch and ran over and hugged Sandra, "Did you come for Thanksgiving?"

"Yes I did."

"Hello?" Lane turned to his daughter as he pulled Sandra's suitcase out of the trunk and set it down.

"Oh, Daddy," Sara hugged her dad. "Thanks. This is going to be a great weekend."

Jenny Hughes stood in the front doorway leaning against the door with her arms folded across her chest. "Well, come on in, dinner is almost ready."

Sandra turned to Sara, "I brought a friend with me, your dad said it was okay."

Sara's face looked puzzled as she looked in the car and saw no one.

Sandra opened the passenger side backdoor and pulled Jerry's cat cage out.

"Oh, Sandra, he's so cute," Sara exclaimed. "Can I pet him?"

"Absolutely, but let's get him inside and settled in first. Can you grab his dish and food, they're on the floor?"

Sandra greeted Jenny and followed Lane into the home. A grand staircase with mahogany steps, posts and rails, accented with white spindles commanded the large foyer. A red Persian rug covered the white and gray stressed marble floor. The entrance was dramatic, yet tasteful. Two sliding doors on the left opened into Lane's study and a stone archway on the right led to the formal dining room. A hall to the right of the staircase led back to the kitchen.

"Sara, would you take Sandra up to the guest room next to mine and help her with Jerry while she unpacks?"

"Yes, Daddy. Come on, Sandra."

"See you in awhile," Lane smiled. Then he followed Jenny, who had started her retreat to the kitchen.

Lane sat down on one of the four stools at the island in the center of the kitchen. Jenny stirred some sauce that was on the stove, her back to him.

"Let that go. Come over and sit with me, we need to talk now."

Jenny picked up the small goblet of Sherry that she always drank as she prepared supper, walked over and sat on the stool next to her son-in-law.

"I want you to give her a chance."

"I—"

"Let me finish, Jenny. She's not anything like the women at the club or the ones we've met at parties. She's real, Mom, just like Annie was, and she makes me happy. I never thought I'd feel happy again, but she has made me happy, and under extraordinary conditions. She's smart, well educated, and articulate. She knows how to handle herself and she's honest, believe me when I tell you, she's honest."

The Return of Sandra Love

"Well, she's beguiled Sara. She's the only thing Sara talked about on the way home. I knew this day would come, but it doesn't make it any easier, Lane."

"Mom, when you lost Bert, I was there for you. Annie talked to me about this at the hospital, she wanted me to be happy. Please, give her a chance."

"I'll try. Why don't you take Sara after dinner and give me some time with her."

"Excellent! Sara and I will clean up and you can talk in the sunroom."

"That's a deal, I like it when you clean up," Jenny smiled wily.

"One thing, she's been through a living hell in the past forty-eight hours. She's an alcoholic who's been dry for over three years. No wine with the lasagna tonight, no alcohol while she's here. The rest you two can talk through."

Jenny stood up and hugged her son-in-law, "Okay."

Lane left and went into his study and phoned his office. He spoke with his administrator, Sharon who was waiting for his call. They went through mail, phone calls, case status and financials. He had her cut back his schedule for the holiday season. Lane finished his call and walked back to the kitchen. Sandra and Sara were finishing setting the table as Jenny was serving the food.

74

"We were just going to call you, Daddy." The four of them sat at the kitchen table.

"Sara, will you say grace?" Jenny asked.

Sara said a short grace, which by her speed, Sandra could tell she repeated often. After dinner Lane offered to clean up and asked Sara to help. Jenny took the cue and invited Sandra to join her for coffee in the sunroom. She led Sandra through a large family room with a huge fireplace. Above the fireplace was a picture of Lane, Annie and Sara when she was about nine. Annie was beautiful, a blonde with a genuine smile, her eyes seemed to twinkle. They stepped into the glass enclosed room and Sandra looked out at the well lit gardens that highlighted the backyard.

"I'll have to take you on a tour while you're here," Jenny offered, "it is really magnificent." The two sat down amidst the potted plants that filled the room. The soft cushioned white wicker chairs were comfortable. Sandra sipped her coffee and then put the mug on the glass-topped matching coffee table that stood between them. Two small lamps on white wicker end tables gave the room warmth.

"Wonderful meal, Miss Jenny."

"Thank you, Sandra. Lane asked me to talk with you tonight, he wants us to get to know each other."

"He doesn't beat around the bush much, does he?"

"No, he's direct and he's honest. He tells me that you are as well."

"Thank you, Miss Jenny, I'll take that as a compliment."

The two women were jousting for position.

"Sandra, please call me Jenny, maybe that will make this conversation less awkward."

"I will, Jenny, but I'm not sure about the second part, let's try."

"Maybe you could slip my shoes on for a mile," Jenny started, "my granddaughter and son-in-law left here Sunday morning to go hunting. Monday night I received a mysterious phone call from Lane asking me to drive down to the coast first thing Tuesday morning. We meet in the parking lot and I drive Sara back and leave Lane with a woman I have never met. On the way home, Sara regales me with her adventure and informs me that there was a dead body in the forest. The next evening Lane comes home, with you, a suitcase and a cat. He promptly sits me down in the kitchen and tells me he likes you and I should give you a chance." Jenny leaned back in her chair. "I'm feeling much less awkward now. How are you doing?"

Sandra smiled, "We're going to be alright, Jenny."

Sandra filled Jenny in on the events of the last three days. The body, the date and her dogs. She shared her back story in general with Jenny. Jenny admired Sandra's frankness and the two women swapped stories with each other over the course of the next two hours. At one point Lane opened the door and asked if he could get them anything, the two women were laughing. Jenny responded to Lane's question, "Go away, Lane, can't you see there are two women bonding here?"

Around 11:30pm, Sara opened the door. "Sandra, are you and Nana going to talk all night?"

"Let's talk more tomorrow," Jenny suggested, "Sandra, it was a pleasure getting to know you. I'll take Sara up now. I'm sure Lane wants a complete briefing as soon as I'm gone. Welcome to our home. I'm glad you're here."

"Thanks, Jenny, I'll see you in the morning. Good night, Sara, let's plan on spending some one-on-one time tomorrow so you and I can get to know each other too."

"That would be great. I can give you the grand tour tomorrow, while Daddy watches football."

A few minutes after the two left, Lane joined Sandra.

"How did it go?"

"No worries. She's a good woman, Lane. I'm glad I came."

"Me too." He reached out and drew Sandra to him. She put her hands around his neck and they kissed, good night.

******

"Jenny, are you sure he's alright there?" Sandra pointed at Jerry, while she peeled potatoes. Jerry had ensconced himself on the top of the island counter."

"I think he looks rather regal there, King Jerry, King of the Kitchen. What do you think, Sara?" Jenny asked.

Sara was leaning on the counter, she gave Jerry another treat and rubbed his head. "Sandra, his eyes are the same color as yours. Is that why you picked him?"

"Yes, I think folks have mentioned that once or thrice, but I didn't pick him, Sara, a friend of mine gave him to me ten years ago. Jerry was a Christmas present."

"Robert Allen?" Jenny asked.

"Yes."

A bellowing roar came from the family room, moments later Lane walked into the kitchen.

"Who's winning?" Sandra asked.

"Bears just won in overtime, ninety-five yard kick-off return to beat the Lions."

"Go Bears!" Sandra cheered.

"Smells great!" Lane commented. "Do you need a taste tester? How long, now?" He walked over and gave Sara a hug as he snaked his arm behind her, picking at the turkey cooling on the counter.

"Oh, Daddy."

"Out!" Jenny ordered.

Lane popped a piece of the bird into his mouth, "Sandra, do you want to call your son and spread the joy?"

"That would be great, if you don't mind? He's at Julie's, the number is in my purse."

"A daughter's a daughter for all of her life; a son is a son until he takes a wife." Jenny recited.

"Isn't that the truth," Sandra smiled. "Have you talked to your parents today?"

"No, they're in Europe. Why don't you use my study." Lane motioned.

"Go." Jenny waved at Sandra, "I'll finish."

Sandra called Tony. They talked for a half an hour, catching up on their lives. Sandra told him about Lane, but not about the circumstances. They talked about Christmas, Tony had been invited to go skiing with Julie and her parents in Vail. He said he would not go if his mom was going to be alone. Sandra gave him a green-light, implying she would be with Lane. She promised she would be up in May for his graduation and that they would play catch-up then. They parted with, "I love you."

******

"Black Friday, who wants to go shopping?" Lane asked as the foursome had breakfast together.

"Me!" Sara raised her hand.

"I've got some shopping I have to do," Jenny raised her hand, "are we talking downtown or the mall."

"Wherever you want," Lane responded.

"Well, we don't want to be party-poopers," Sandra held Jerry in her lap and she raised his paw.

"Speaking of parties, we have one at the club tomorrow night. Did you bring a dress?" Lane asked.

"I didn't."

"Not you Sandra, I was asking Jerry." Lane smiled.

"I think we are both dress-less."

"Sandra, I'll help you pick one out," Sara volunteered.

"That sounds like fun, Sara."

The Crabtree Valley Mall opened in 1972. The mall had over 1.3 million square feet of shopping including the Belk Department store that was one of the anchors. It offered high-end shopping at exclusive retail stores with plenty of parking for shoppers in the Raleigh area. It was located on Glenwood Ave, inside the I-440 Beltline.

"So where are we going first?" Lane asked as they entered the mall.

"Belk's!" Sara shouted.

"How about I meet you at the food court at 1pm?" Jenny asked.

"Jenny, no, please come with us," Sandra pleaded.

Jenny gave Sandra a hug and whispered, "This is your time, hon. Go bond." She kissed Sandra on the cheek.

"Thanks."

Jenny headed off to do her shopping.

The three walked down the mall, Lane in the middle holding Sara's and Sandra's hands. "Why do women do that?"

Sandra looked at him. "You don't know?"

"You do?"

"Sure."

"I'm all ears," Lane said, "please educate me."

"It's how we're raised, Lane. Guys play sports where scoring a touchdown or making a basket is the goal. Girls play with dolls, have tea parties and talk on the phone. Why are we here today?"

"To buy you a dress." Lane answered.

"Me too, Daddy!" Sara added.

"Sara, what are we doing today?"

Shopping... Sara sung the word.

"There ya go, Lane. Men are goal oriented, women are process oriented. You're here to buy a dress. Sara, Jenny and I are going ... *shopping...*" Sandra sung the last word.

"Well this is an epiphany."

In the dress department Sara tried on a couple of dresses, she couldn't find anything she liked. "Sandra, why don't you try on some dresses," she suggested in frustration.

"Go ahead, Sandra," Lane coaxed her.

"Okay, give me a minute." Sandra walked over to the front of the women's department and looked at a mannequin that was wearing a black cocktail dress with full shoulder sleeves, a scooped neckline and a flowing skirt hemmed just above the knee. She reached into the rack and pulled out a size four.

"I'll try this one." Sandra took the dress into the dressing room as Sara sat on a cushioned settee next to her father. A few moments later Sandra emerged.

"Wow!" Lane gasped.

"It's beautiful, Sandra," Sara added.

"That looks like it was made for you, dear," the saleswoman that was helping them commented.

"Daddy, can I try one on?"

"Sara, that might be a little old for you."

Sara whispered, "Daddy, I'm not going to look like Sandra, please."

"What do you think, Sandra?"

"I think you should let her try it on and then decide."

"What size are you, hon?" The saleswoman asked.

"Size two."

"I hope we have a two left."

"Try the one on the mannequin." Sandra told her as she sat down on the settee next to Lane.

Several minutes later, the saleswoman returned with the dress.

"Size two," she smiled.

Sara disappeared into the dressing rooms. When she walked out, her face was beaming. She twirled around as Lane sat and wondered where his little girl had gone.

"You are quite stunning, Sara. Do you like it?"

"Daddy!"

"We'll take both, on my account, Fran," Lane told the saleswoman.

"Lane, you don't have to—"

"I told you Tuesday night," he lowered his voice, "it's been a long time since I made a woman happy. Allow me this."

Sandra felt uncomfortable, as this was reminiscent of her life in Chicago, but she acquiesced to Lane's request and then hugged his arm.

"We can be twins tomorrow night, Sandra," Sara was still excited over their find, "but first we need to accessorize."

"Here we go!" Lane stood up and offered Sandra his hand. She giggled as he pulled her up off the settee and followed Sara to the shoe department.

******

The Carolina Country Club was located on Glenwood Ave a few blocks north of Lane's home. It was over seventy years old. It was one of the symbols of old money inside the beltline; golf course, tennis courts, swimming pool, and wealth. Lane pulled up in front of the club house and got out of the Mercedes as two attendants opened the passenger side doors.

"Good evening, Mr. Brendel," one of them greeted Lane as he helped Jenny out of the car.

"Good evening, John." Lane walked around the front of the vehicle as first Sara and then Sandra stepped out of the back of the car. The two looked like twins, same dress, shawl, shoes and purse, and they both wore gold stud earrings and a small gold cross necklace. The four walked up the steps and into the clubhouse.

Susan Sterling Ballew was hosting the party and greeted them at the ballroom entrance. She was the quintessential southern belle.

"Good evening, Lane," she greeted the party, "Miss Jenny, Sara." She looked at Sandra and then back to Sara. "You look quite grown up tonight, Sara," her saccharine smile evident to all.

"Thank you."

"Susan, I'd like to introduce you to Sandra Horne, she's staying with us for the holiday."

"It's nice to meet you, Miss Horne, a friend of Lane's?"

Before Sandra could answer, Jenny responded, "Sandra is a friend of, ours."

Sandra understood that language as she smiled demurely.

Taken back, Susan hesitated a moment and then composed herself, "Hope you all have a wonderful evening."

The beautiful ballroom had tables on carpet surrounding a wood dance floor under a huge crystal chandelier; at the far end a band was playing Glenn Miller's "Moonlight Serenade."

They were seated at a table with Douglas J. McKinney, a federal judge and his wife, and another young attorney, who worked for Lane, Judson Post and his wife, Michelle. Sandra sat between Lane and Sara. Dinner was served at 7pm and as the evening went on, couples ventured out onto the dance floor. Lane asked Sandra, "Do you waltz?"

"Not really."

"Good, neither do I, we'll fake it." He stood up and pulled Sandra's chair out.

They walked hand-in-hand onto the dance floor.

"Am I on display?"

"You bet. We'll make the front page of society news tomorrow."

Sandra laughed.

The Return of Sandra Love

Court Street

Saturday night around 10:30pm, she took a break. She stepped outside and down the steps as she lit a cigarette, "I need a break from those people in there."

It was one of those typical North Carolina November nights, the overnight low could be anywhere from the fifties to the thirties. She didn't know, she hadn't caught the weather report Saturday, too busy getting ready for Saturday night. She had draped a shawl over her shoulders and the night air was chilly, but refreshing. She walked down the concrete, to the intersection, she looked up at the clear night sky. "That's beautiful," she murmured, as she looked up at the blanket of stars that filled the southern sky.

A car came down the street and stopped beside her. The driver reached over and rolled the passenger side window down. A nice looking middle age man was behind the wheel, "Pardon me Miss, but can you help me, I'm looking for a place called 'Evelyn's.' Do you know if I'm even close?"

"Evelyn's is right down there, third building on the right. Why are you going there?"

"Listen Miss, no offense, but I don't know you from Adam. As far as I know, you could be a mugger or a cop. I just needed to know where it was, thank you." He started to roll the window back up.

"Wait a minute, I'm not a mugger and I sure as hell am not a cop. You looking for a good time, sugar?"

"I am, if it's quick. I was in a bar and two young Marines were talking about dropping by later. My wife's out with her girlfriends, so when they gave me the directions, I thought I'd come over and check it out."

"Why don't you check this out first?" She bent over and put her forearms on the car's window ledge, her low cut dress showed off her cleavage in the window.

"Very nice, are you a working girl?"

"Honey, I'm a professional."

"How much?"

"For what?"

"A blowjob."

"Wife kind of prudish, huh?" The man didn't respond. "Fifty."

"The Marines told me the price was twenty five."

"We ain't at Evelyn's, hon."

"Okay, I'll go thirty five, or I go to Evelyn's."

"That's a deal." She tried to open the door to get in, but it was locked. "Can you unlock the door?"

"Not until you open the purse and I get a good look inside."

"What the hell mister?"

"His voice remained calm, "Look Miss, if you're a cop or you have a gun in there, I could get arrested or killed. Open the purse, I wouldn't ask you to do this if we were at Evelyn's."

"Here!" She opened the purse, she was clearly miffed, "Satisfied?"

"Okay, hop in," he reached across and unlocked the door.

She got in, "Thirty five bucks please," she held out her hand.

He reached into his front coat pocket and took out some cash, he separated a twenty, a ten and a five from the rest of the bills. He looked over at her, "You're not going to take this and jump out of the car are you?"

She busted up laughing, "First you don't want me to get in, then you don't want me to get out. Stop worrying, sugar, tonight you're going to get your money's worth."

He smiled, "What's your name?"

"Deedee."

The Return of Sandra Love

"Okay, Deedee, where are we going?"

"Down the street and around the corner, there's a small park at the end of the street."

The car pulled into the unlit park and stopped.

The young woman leaned down on the car's bench seat and unbuckled the man's belt, "Okay, honey, scoot them down."

He raised up off the bench seat and pushed his pants and underwear down to his thighs. She went down on his flaccid penis and took it into her mouth. She started to rub with her right hand while her mouth went up and down his member. As she did, he placed his left hand gently on top of her head and reached up with his right hand and pulled down a plastic bag that was wedged above the sun-visor. He removed a cloth from the bag. Suddenly, he grabbed her hair with his left hand and pulled her head up twisting it toward the steering wheel. The cloth went over her nose and mouth quickly.

"Whaaa—Mphhh..." the woman tried to get up, but he was too strong and the big man leaned forward and pinned her between his body and the steering wheel. She kicked her legs and tried to scream, as she did, she breathed in the deadly fumes. She dug her long nails into his hand, in the dark car she hadn't noticed he was wearing black leather gloves. Her eyes bulged and filled with tears as fear overwhelmed her. She pulled at his hand, but the cloth never moved. The struggle was brief, slowly her body relaxed as her eyes rolled up and her arms went limp at her sides. He kept the cloth over her face for a few minutes as her breathing became rhythmic, then he pushed her up and she sagged into the passenger door. He placed the cloth back in the bag and pulled his trousers up. The driver's door opened and the man got out of the car and looked around, the park was deserted. He walked around and opened the rear passenger door, then the front passenger door. She tumbled out and into his arms. He lifted her out and deposited her limp body face down on the back seat, her short mini-skirt rode up over her butt. He removed his gloves and threw them on the floor. He took three cable ties out of his coat pocket and bound her wrists and elbows behind her back, then he strapped her ankles together. He pushed her face down on the floor, closed both doors, walked around the car and sat down behind the wheel. He pushed the bench seat back pinning her on the floor. The car pulled out of the park. They had not been there ten minutes.

He muttered to himself, "Whores."

******

Sunday was a day of rest. Lane, Jenny, Sara and Sandra attended services and ate breakfast out. When they returned to the house, Lane settled in front of the television watching football. Sara received a call from her best girlfriend Lynda, and went over to her house for a sleep over. She attended a private academy in

Raleigh and was off school until Wednesday.
Jenny, Sandra and Jerry walked in the gardens
and Jenny showed Sandra her spacious
apartment over the garage. Then they spent
time talking in the sunroom.

"You and Lane have known each other for a
week. Where do you see your relationship
going, Sandra?"

"What a great question, Jenny, I don't have a
clue. I've always been a pretty practical person,
Lane and I live in two different worlds. There's
no way he can live in mine, my trailer's the size
of your kitchen."

Jenny smiled.

"And I have a good picture of his world from
these last few days, I don't think it would work
for me. Right now, we are both lonely and
vulnerable, I enjoy his company and he enjoys
mine. Maybe I could just use him for sex?"

Jenny laughed out loud.

"I've done the mistress thing, I don't care for it
much and I've told Lane, I haven't been lucky
with love. Got any ideas?"

"Oh no, you two are on your own," Jenny waved
her finger as she chuckled.

"Are you worried about Sara?"

"I don't know, should I be? You're a smart
woman, Sandra, neither one of us wants to see
her hurt."

"That would never be my intent."

"I know that," Jenny acknowledged, "but you
know there's a difference between intent and
effect."

"Yes, that's true. How old is she?"

"She'll turn fifteen in three weeks, on the
twentieth."

Sandra looked out the windows as she reflected,
"Fifteen was not my best year," she said softly
as she remembered her rape, "you know you
have about one more year with her. After they
get their license, they're, gone baby gone. "

"Yes, I remember Annie at sixteen, she loved
driving and Elvis," Jenny looked pensive.

The two sat quietly for a few moments, then
Sandra offered, "Jenny, I lost my mom two years
ago on Christmas eve, I miss her very much,
she was smart and strong. You remind me of
her."

Jenny looked at Sandra, "What are you saying,
Sandra?"

"Lane and I are looking for love, Sara's looking
for a mother figure, you've lost your daughter
and I've lost my mom. What do you think?"

"Well, all the puzzle pieces are there, guess we'd just have to put them together."

"Let's make a pact."

"What kind of pact?" Jenny asked.

"That we will keep each other in the loop."

"Deal." Jenny held out her hand, they shook on it.

"That's quite a grip you've got, Jenny."

The three of them had left-over turkey and fixings for dinner. When dinner was over Sandra offered to do the dishes and clean up. Jenny took the cue and retired to her apartment. Sandra finished and curled up with Lane on the sectional sofa in the family room as he watched the end of the game.

"Seems you and Jenny had some quality time together today."

"Yes, we came to an accord."

"I like it when you use big words, it makes me hot." They were spooning on the sofa and he wrapped his right arm around her and caressed her breasts. He started to kiss her neck.

"You're incorrigible!" Sandra feigned an attempt to push him away.

"Oh that's it, keep talking, big SAT words."

Sandra turned over and put her arms around his neck, she pushed her breasts into his chest. She gave him a smoky look with her big green eyes and batted her eye lashes, then she kissed him passionately on the mouth. In a few moments, Lane was ready to go. Sandra cut the kiss off. She opened her mouth and licked his neck, then she breathed gently in his ear and whispered, "I'm not being pedantic am I? That would be so jejune."

Lane knew when he'd been had. "That's enough, I'm taking you to my bed!" He stood up, he was as stiff as a board. He picked her up in his arms while she playfully pounded her fists into his chest.

Sandra giggled, "You animal!"

******

Monday morning found the two of them in bed. They had made love several times and talked in between before they fell off to sleep. Sandra had agreed to stay until Wednesday, when Sara went back to school, then Lane would drive her home. A little before 9am they came down for juice and coffee, Lane in sweat pants and a NC State tee-shirt and Sandra in his bathrobe.

"You're up late this morning, everyone alright?" Jenny asked, as if she had no idea about last night.

"Right as rain," Lane answered as he poured two mugs of coffee from the pot Jenny had brewed.

"I think Lane was up late last night, he was studying for a vocabulary test he has today," Sandra baited him.

"Ignore her, Mom," he responded with a smile as he handed Sandra her coffee and then tousled her hair.

"Lane, this is my bridge club day, I'll be leaving in about an hour and should be back around 4pm. I'll pick up Sara."

"Okay, Mom, thanks." Lane had already started to read the newspaper.

The phone rang. Jenny answered it, "Lane, it's for you."

Lane took the phone. "Hello...yes it is...fine thank you. What's up? Good...yes, she's here...today?...what time?...what's the address?" Lane wrote on a pad next to the phone. "Okay, we'll see you at 1pm." He hung up.

"Who was that?" Sandra asked.

"Derrick Strong. He has the medical examiner's results and they've identified the body. He's at the state crime lab here in Raleigh, Mac Farmer is with him. They want to meet with us at 1pm."

"Us?"

"Yes. He asked me to be sure to bring you."

The state crime lab was located on Garner Street in Raleigh. Lane and Sandra were escorted to a conference room and a few minutes later Strong and Farmer joined them. Each of them carried a file.

"Thanks for coming in." Derrick Strong began as the two agents sat down at the conference table. "Her name was Loretta Smith, originally from Greenville. Several priors for shoplifting and petty theft. More recently, solicitation and prostitution. She was twenty two. We've notified family, just her mother. There's been a leak, the press has the story, we have a press conference at 4pm, it will make the news tonight."

"What's the lab have?" Lane asked.

"We have latent on the tire tracks, he came in a car, not a truck. We'd have to find the vehicle before we could match."

"And the footprints?" Sandra asked.

"The prints in the forest match the ones at your trailer, Sandra. You were right about his size, prints are size thirteen wide. Our thinking is that he passed the fire trail a couple of times on Rte 24 last Monday. When he saw the deputy posted at the entrance, he swung around and caught you and Lane coming out the Star Hill Drive trail and followed you home."

"You might want to rethink that, Derrick. How long had she been dead?"

"Tough call, but they think no more than forty eight hours. What part do you want us to rethink?"

"He was in the forest Monday, watching us, that's why he killed my dogs. He was sending me a message about helping you."

"Sandra, he wouldn't have had enough time to get out of the forest, onto Rte 24 and swing around to the Star Hill Drive trail to follow you and Lane. If he didn't follow you, how did he know where you..."

"*Duh*," Sandra stared at Strong.

"This guy knows you!"

"Welcome to small town south, Agent Strong, where everyone knows everyone." All three men looked at Sandra. "Here's my two cents. If she was working, he probably picked her up Friday or Saturday night. He wouldn't have taken her into the forest during daylight, not in hunting season. He took her in Saturday or Sunday night. He knows the forest well. He lives in an isolated area, he couldn't have done that to her in a neighborhood, too risky, and it was probably done outside. How about trace evidence, no semen, right?"

"None," Strong answered. "How did you know?"

"This is not a sexual thing for him. This is some kind of righteous indignity thing he has in his head."

"You mean like his mother was a whore and he's seeking revenge for a neglected childhood? Farmer asked. "Lane, that sounds like something up your alley."

"This guy wouldn't have a chance in court, unless he pleaded insanity," Lane replied tersely. "I don't do insanity defenses."

Sandra responded to Farmer, "Whores, sluts, whatever label you want to put on those types of women, but usually they're just women of low moral character and high sexual drive, like a lot of men I've known. Our society doesn't call those men whores or sluts, we call them studs and for some unknown reason, they're admired. Men seem to have placed all the moral weight of our society squarely on the shoulders of women, don't ya think, Mac?"

"Sandra, I didn't mean—"

"Don't worry about your comment, moral women think the same way you do. But just for future reference, the difference between a whore and a prostitute is, a whore does it for free, a prostitute gets paid, in the business they're called working girls."

"Okay, thanks for the lesson," Farmer's face reflected disinterest, he looked tired.

"Sandra, we've been busting hump for the last week. We went to the top brass to get the lab results fast. I guess we're a bit tired, and we have this press conference at 4pm. We want you to know, we appreciate your help," Strong interjected.

"If I were you, I'd try and find out where she was working, it's been a week, no one has reported her missing?" Sandra asked.

"Sheriff Baker has nothing and there's nothing on BOLO," Mac told her.

"What's BOLO?"

"It's a system we have, the acronym stands for 'Be On the Look Out,' it helps local law enforcement with missing persons before they enter the NCIC system," Farmer continued.

"NCIC?" Sandra remained puzzled.

"National Crime Information Center, it's the feds system."

Sandra looked at Farmer, "Okay, thanks for the lesson. Are we done?"

Farmer smiled, "Not quite," he looked at Strong.

"Sandra, some of the prints Brent lifted in your trailer were yours. When he ran them, they came up in a secure file with a reference number. I spoke to Eric Marsh this morning.

Lane, could we speak to Sandra privately for a few minutes?" Strong asked.

Lane started to stand up.

"Where are you going? Sandra asked.

Lane looked puzzled, "The men's room?"

"Sit," a wry smile crossed Sandra's face, "Lane is my attorney, whatever you have to say, you can say it in front of Lane. We have no secrets. Isn't that right, counselor?"

"Right as rain," Lane sat down.

Strong leaned forward in his chair, "He briefed me on your adventure in Tennessee back in the seventies. He told me that you were the best he's ever worked with, you come highly recommended."

"For what?" Sandra asked.

"Mac," Derrick looked at Farmer.

"Sandra, we think we know where she worked, a place in Jacksonville on Court Street. When you think Court Street, think Times Square. It's run by a woman named Evelyn from New York City, hard as nails, and hates cops, but she's real friendly in political circles, if you follow my drift."

"I follow. What are you asking?"

"Will you help us? We know you're not in the business anymore, but you know the business better than we do and you're not a cop. We need a lead here."

"You want to involve me in this after what he did to my dogs?"

"It's your call, Sandra, but we'd appreciate anything you can do."

"I'll let you know," Sandra stood up. "One more thing. Did they find anything in her lungs, ether or chloroform trace?"

"Ether, how the hell did you know?" Strong asked.

Sandra smiled, "Elementary Watson, if he picked her up in Jacksonville, he needed to transport her to wherever his place is; drugs are quicker and more effective than rope and gags. They're used by men who traffick women."

Evelyn's

Wednesday morning Sandra said her good-byes to Sara and Jenny. She and Lane got into his Jeep and drove back to her trailer. Lane wanted to put her up in a hotel, but she argued that she would be on her alert now that she knew there was a killer out there watching her. She told Lane she actually felt safer in the forest.

"Think of this as my Fortress of Solitude, Lane. Like Superman's."

"You're not going to get involved in this thing are you, Sandra?"

"A week ago I made a vow about this." Sandra's voice was very calm, "This guy wants to come in to my house and push me around? You played football for NC State, how well would the Wolfpack take that?"

"Not well," Lane admitted, "but you're not the Wolfpack, Sandra."

She smiled, "You're right, Lane. My defense is stronger, my offense is more deadly and he wants to play in my house?"

Lane shook his head, "Be careful, please."

"I promise."

"When will I see you again? Weekends?"

"I don't want to take weekend time away from you and Sara. Jenny gave me your card and home number, I'll call, we'll work something out. How's Christmas sound?"

"It sounds like three weeks."

"Absence makes—"

Lane grabbed her and kissed her long, when he was done, "Hold on to that until I see you again."

"I will," Sandra watched him as he walked out her path and disappeared.

Sandra went shopping Thursday at the Piggly Wiggly store in Cape Carteret. The newspaper and TV stations had covered the press conference in Raleigh. Everyone was talking about the body in the woods, the murder. Someone had leaked information on the crime scene and the press had a juicy, *if it bleeds it leads* story.

"Sandra!"

Sandra looked up, Claire-Anne Bolt pushed her shopping cart up the aisle, "Where have you been, girlfriend?"

"I was with Lane in Raleigh for the holiday weekend."

"That guy is not hard to look at. Have you seen the paper?"

"I was going to pick one up on the way out."

"Here, take mine."

Sandra read the article. It was specific on the victim's name, her home town and the efforts the police were taking to try to identify any one who may have known her or her whereabouts prior to her death. The cause of death was given as multiple stab wounds. No specific information was given about the crime scene, but contact information was included. Sandra looked up as she finished the article.

"Rare for these parts," Claire-Anne commented.

"She was awfully young to die like that," Sandra responded.

"What are you doing for the holidays, Sandra?" Claire-Anne switched subjects.

"I'll be in Raleigh."

"Hope to see you before you go. Are you going to Big Ben's Christmas party?"

"When is it this year?"

"The thirteenth, a week from Saturday."

"At the VFW Post in Cedar Point?"

"Yep, same as last year. We can pick you up if you need a lift."

"That's really sweet, Claire-Anne. My truck's running fine. What time does it start?"

"Same as last year, 7pm."

"Okay, I'll see you then if not before," the two hugged, "and thanks again for your help last week with Sara."

"No problem."

******

Evelyn Martin was a rough looking woman with a muscular build. In her prime she would have been considered voluptuous, but at fifty eight years old she referred to herself as a big bone girl. She knew how to handle herself both physically and politically. She had worked for the mob in New York City. She had managed a porn theater, a string of adult book stores, an escort service and two brothels. She also controlled the flow of street walkers in Times Square through a network of pimps who worked for her. Evelyn dressed well, in the right light she could pass for forty, but she used too much make-up and in the wrong light it cheapened her look. Her hair was dyed dark black. Her real name was Sophia Crocetti, she was Italian through and through. She and her husband never had children. He had been with the mob since he was eighteen, he was shot to death in a drug deal in 1974. Evelyn picked up stakes and moved south with a Marine she had met in the city.

Luigi's was the best Italian food on the coast, it was two blocks from Evelyn's brothel off Court Street. She ate lunch there every day, but

Evelyn's

Sunday, Sunday her business was closed.
Friday, December 5, was no exception. She
entered the restaurant around 11:45am and sat
at her usual booth in the back, facing the front
door. After ordering her meal, the waiter brought
a bottle of Opus One Red Bordeaux to the table.

"Miss Evelyn, the lady at the far table wishes
you try this with your meal."

Evelyn looked at the two hundred dollar bottle of
wine, then she looked toward the front of the
restaurant. The sun coming through the front
doors and windows silhouetted the woman she
had passed when she arrived. Evelyn turned to
the waiter, "Tony, ask the lady if she will join me.
Bring another glass."

The waiter walked to the other table and spoke
with the woman. Evelyn reached into her purse
and pulled out a cigarette and lighter, she placed
them on the table. She removed a .22 caliber
derringer and placed it in her lap, as the woman
approached her table. She was dressed in a
black business jacket over a white camisole and
a miniskirt that exposed her legs to mid-thigh.
She wore large black sunglasses and a wide-
brimmed, black fedora.

"Please, sit down," Evelyn extended her left
hand toward the low-back bench across from
her.

"Thank you."

Evelyn picked up her cigarette and lit it with her gold Cartier single flame butane lighter. The woman slipped her black shoulder strap purse off her shoulder and reached into the purse. Evelyn turned the derringer in her lap toward the woman. The woman removed a cigarette and lit it with the exact lighter Evelyn had used. She took a drag on the cigarette and blew the smoke across the table at Evelyn.

"You going to shoot me, Evey? You don't like my choice of wines?"

Evelyn looked at her, "No one's called me Evey in fifteen years," Do I know you?"

The woman turned her hand around exposing her lighter, then she removed her sunglasses.

Evelyn looked at the lighter and then at those big green eyes, "I know you...damn it...Sandra, Sam's Sandra...Sandra Love!"

"How ya been, hon?" Sandra smiled.

"What the hell are you doing in Jacksonville, North Carolina?"

"I'm having lunch with my friend Evelyn."

"You're damn right you are!" Both women slid out of the booth and hugged. It had been over fifteen years since they had met while Sandra was in New York with Sam. They had hit it off from the start. Their patrons had taken them shopping at Tiffany's where they had bought the women the matching lighters. The two settled back into the booth.

"This isn't a coincidence is it, Sandra?"

"No it's not, Evey, and I'll explain, but first, let's catch up."

The two women talked for a while catching up on the years. Sandra told her she had left the life and put herself through college before going to work in banking, meeting her second husband and moving to the area. She went on to tell her about her husband's injury, their divorce and her new relationship with a lawyer who lived in Raleigh. She told her that he was an avid hunter and that while they were hunting together, they had come across the body. She filled her in on the last week including the slaughter of her dogs and her trip to Raleigh. She told Evelyn that when the cops identified the body and looked at Loretta Smith's arrest record, they also shared with Sandra their opinion that she may have worked for Evelyn at her place in Jacksonville.

"When they told me that the madam's name was Evelyn, she was from New York City and she was hard as nails, I knew it had to be you."

"So, you're here as a *toady* for the cops, Sandra?"

Sandra leaned into the table, "What have I ever done to you, Evey, that you would treat me with such disrespect?"

Evelyn recoiled, she realized she was not talking to the twenty something young woman she knew fifteen years ago, "Nothing, Sandra, and I apologize. The comment was uncalled for, just tell me why you're here?"

The waiter came to the table and opened the wine. Evelyn ordered Veal Parmesan and Sandra followed suit. The waiter took the order and left.

Sandra lowered her voice, "I'm here because there's a weirdo out there that thinks I'm helping the police and someone needs to catch or kill the son of a bitch before he kills me or someone else. This guy is a real freak, Evey, he likes to cut them up and he's big, real big. Ring any bells?"

"No, but I'll ask my girls. It may be too late, Sandra."

"What do you mean?"

"I had another girl disappear last Saturday night."

"Talk to me, Evey."

"Her name was Deedee and she was pretty street smart, Sandra. Much smarter than Butterfly."

"Was that Loretta Smith's working name?"

Evelyn's

"Yes, she was really light and airy, a sweet kid, but naive, too trusting for the business."

"Why didn't you report her missing?"

"They come and go at that age, Sandra, they fall in love and they're gone, most of the time they don't even take their stuff with them. What was I going to do, call the cops and tell them one of my working girls was missing?"

"What about this Deedee?"

"No, she was too experienced, it would take some doing to con her."

"If another body shows up, Evey, the shit is going to hit the fan."

"I know, I've got some political support and two local cops on payroll, but it's not like working in New York, no *family* down here. They have SBI agents here in town, we don't get along. I'm open for suggestions."

"Well, they want my help. I could act as a liaison, but if you have nothing to give them?"

"I understand," Evelyn sipped her wine, "Delicious, you haven't touched your wine?"

"I don't drink anymore, Evey."

"Good for you. I remember you could hold your own with the best of them."

"Not anymore. Do you have any security cameras in your place?"

"No, I have two ex-marines that watch the girls, they're big and bad."

"Buy some, and make sure you have a face cam at the door and some field cameras that cover the outside."

"Why don't you come show me after lunch?"

"Sure, do you have a picture of Deedee?"

"Yes."

"Good. Tell me about your house, how long have you been here, how many girls, what their backgrounds are, any incidents or ongoing problems?" Sandra asked.

"I have a good ethnic mix, most of which are former Marine wives. Asians, from Vietnam, the Philippines and Japan; two black girls from South Carolina; three Hispanics and the rest are white girls, mostly from the south. I opened up four years ago after I crossed some local palms. We've had a few incidents, but it's the normal stuff, abusive drunks, jealous suitors and occasionally an ex-husband; nothing my bouncers couldn't handle onsite. This is the south Sandra, I teach the girls customer service and good manners, it goes a long way down here, you know that."

"You were always good with your girls, Evey. Do they still call you *Momma Rabbit*? "

"Yes, I always liked it, so I kept it. I'll talk to my girls tonight. You said this guy was big, how big? Do you have any other description besides big?"

"From where he hung her on the trees, I'd say he was at least 6'5" maybe taller. Evey, he carried her over a mile into the forest. This guy's big and strong, but that's all they have."

"Hell, Sandra, there's over thirty thousand Marines on base and just about all of them can hump a mile with heavy weight on their back."

"True, but how many of them wear a size thirteen shoe?"

Evelyn nodded. The two finished their lunch and left.

The man sat in his car in the restaurant's parking lot as Sandra and Evelyn walked out of Luigi's and down the street toward her brothel.

"Whores," he whispered as he gripped the knife on the seat next to him tighter.

The Return of Sandra Love

Small Town South

The Cape Carteret Community Watch was an organization that started in 1976. The group worked in cooperation with the Cape Carteret police force and had an office in the police station equipped with radio communications for drivers making rounds. Their primary role was to make rounds in the town of Cape Carteret and report any suspicious activity, particularly for non-occupied vacation homes after the owners had registered with the group. The CCCW also had a social function. The group met on the second Friday of the month at 6pm in the Western Park Community Center. The town's mayor and the chief of police attended the meetings, it gave them an opportunity to interact socially with members, brief them on current town issues and listen to a guest speaker invited by the group. The meeting also included a pot-luck dinner prepared by the members.

Claire-Anne Bolt was the current president. While December's meeting was normally dinner, a brief presentation from the mayor, and an exchange of gifts among the members, Friday December 12, was an exception. Pressure from town residents had forced all the commissioners to attend and share their views on the recent event, the danger to the community and what the town was doing to protect the citizenry.

Claire-Anne opened the meeting with a Pledge of Allegiance and a short prayer, then they all sat down for supper. A prominent business man in town, Big Ben Taylor was holding an open discussion at his table about what should be done. Ben Taylor was a wealthy landowner who had helped develop the Crystal Coast area. When the meal was over, Claire-Anne had the Treasurer's report read, the Secretary's minutes of the last meeting approved, and then asked Chief Briggs to present the latest on the ongoing investigation.

As the chief began to speak, one of the town's police officers walked into the building and up to the chief, pulling him aside. He whispered into the chief's ear as the group waited. The chief motioned to the mayor and the three men huddled for a few moments. Then the chief and the officer left the meeting.

Mayor Dave Donnelly addressed the room, "The chief had to leave due to an emergency, I'll try to answer any questions you have."

Ben Taylor stood up, "I have a question, Dave, what emergency could be more important than this meeting?"

"They've found another body, it's inside the town limits."

The room exploded with voices.

******

The man walked slowly down the dark path toward Sandra's trailer. He reached the ridge where he could see the trailer on the opposite ridge, the lights were on and Sandra's silhouette could be seen through the thin curtains as she moved around in the kitchen. He walked down the trail, across the bridge and up the hill to the yard in front of her home. The forest was cold and windy as a cold front set in across the Crystal Coast.

"Sandra!" He shouted.

"Who's out there?" The voice shouted back from inside the trailer.

"It's me, Mac Farmer, Can I come in?"

The door opened. Sandra stood in the shadows with her .45 pointed at Farmer's chest.

"Okay?" Farmer asked as he raised his empty hands.

"Come on in. What brings you out on a night like this?"

The SBI agent stepped into the trailer, he was dressed for the outdoor weather, "There's another body in the forest, behind the golf course."

Sandra's mouth grimaced, "Have you been there?"

"Yes, Strong is there with some locals from the Cape Carteret police. He asked me to pick you up. We have some weather coming in, will you help?"

"Let me get dressed." Sandra walked over to the hall closet, put the gun on an end table and pulled out her green parka. "How's it look?"

"This is worse than the first one, he really worked her over good."

"Is she hanging?"

"Same as the first."

"Who found her?"

"A couple out walking their dog. They're both pretty badly shaken. Their home is just a few hundred yards from the site. It's going to be hard to keep a lid on this."

Sandra slid a holster onto her belt and picked up the .45.

"Got a permit to carry that?"

"You bet!" Sandra holstered the weapon.

The two left the trailer and walked back to Farmer's car. He drove the 1976 Plymouth Grand Fury down Rte 58 with his blue dashboard light flashing and siren off. They turned onto Taylor Notion Road and then left onto Star Hill Drive. They passed the airstrip alongside the golf course and a hundred yards ahead were a half dozen vehicles parked on the side of the road. One of Cape Carteret's police officers stood in the road stopping and checking the occasional car that came along. Several flare sticks lit up the road and the officer's patrol car had its flashing lights on. Farmer pulled off the road and the two walked into the woods on a narrow footpath.

Derrick Strong stood on the edge of the trees outside the yellow tape protecting the crime scene; twenty feet behind him, the naked, bloody body of a young woman was nailed to two trees.

"Sandra, thank you for coming," Strong greeted them.

"Where's Brent? Is he en route?" She asked.

"Yes, but he was at the lab in Raleigh and we have a deteriorating weather situation here. We were hoping you might take a look around. If there's anything you can do before this front hits, we'd appreciate it."

"I think we can rule out anything on the footpath, looks like everybody and his brother came in that way."

"That's not a shot at my men, is it?"

Sandra turned around, Chief Briggs was standing behind her, "No chief, just an observation."

"Do you really think she can help us here?" The chief asked Farmer as he pointed at Sandra. "Can't we at least get the body down from there. We can't have her hanging there in the morning! We're thirty yards from the green on the fifth hole, there will be golfers out here as soon as this front blows through. If we want to know who she is, let's take her down and run her prints." He shouted as it started to rain and the wind whipped across the golf course and into the trees.

Farmer responded, "Calm down, George, we'll have her out by morning."

"Give me your flashlight, Mac." Sandra pointed the flashlight at the corpse slowly moving the light up and down as she approached the body. The men moved in behind her. She studied the body for a few moments. "What do you see?" Sandra asked.

Strong responded, "He beat this one, before he cut her up. There are bruises all over her face and body, her breasts and ribs, in addition to the cuts."

"Look carefully at the bruises, are they all alike?" Sandra asked. She stepped in close to the body and bent down, shining the flashlight up into the corpse's face. She pulled something out of her parka, looked at it and then back at the body.

Strong inspected the bruises on the body. "Sandra, they're all different, I don't see...wait a minute..." He moved his flashlight up and down the lifeless body. "Some of these are yellowed out, much older than others. The bastard took his time with her, probably over a few days."

"Good, and..." Sandra led him on.

"You were right about him living in an isolated area, like a farm or a hunting camp," Farmer interjected.

Strong thought out loud, "He doesn't use them sexually, so why would you do this to a woman?"

"Come on Derrick, you're almost there. If it's not sexual, what's the purpose of torture?"

"Punishment...or information...or confession..."

"Who takes confessions, Derrick? I'll give you a hint, working girls see them from time to time, but they're always shocked when they do."

"You think he's a man of God, a priest or a pastor, don't you!" Strong growled.

"Maybe, maybe not, but I'd bet my ass he's doing this to save their souls. He's doing God's work. He tortures them like the inquisition did and then when they repent, he dispatches their souls off to heaven. He hangs them up like Christ on the cross, martyrs. He's sending a message alright, repent or die. Trust me on this, Derrick, I know what I'm talking about."

"Sandra, your whole theory is based on the assumption this woman was a prostitute. We need to find out who she is first, then we can start theorizing."

"Her name is Dorothy Huggins, she was twenty eight. She worked under the name Deedee, at Evelyn's. She disappeared last Saturday night. Here's her picture." Sandra pulled the picture of Dorothy Huggins, that Evelyn gave her, out of her parka. She handed it to him, "You said you wanted my help?"

"Yes."

"Trust me."

"You went to Evelyn's behind my back?"

"If I was behind your back, Derrick, it's because I have your back. That's got to be a reciprocal relationship, understand?" Sandra walked away from Strong shining the flashlight on the ground behind the body as the rain started to come down hard.

Mac walked up to Strong, "What do you think, Derrick?"

"I think Eric Marsh was right. She's good, but we need to talk to her."

"Good luck with that, pal."

As Sandra looked around the woods, Brent Wilkes walked up the footpath carrying his black bag. "I got here as fast as I could," he stepped inside the yellow tape as he looked up at the body. "Not going to be much here that's not corrupted now with this weather. Is that Sandra over there?"

"Yes," Farmer answered.

"Let me talk to her, you've got other problems."

"What problems?" Strong asked.

"The press and TV reporters are here."

"Oh shit!" The chief responded.

"George, can you deal with that?" Farmer asked. "Tell them we'll have a press conference tomorrow with whatever we can share, and check on the medical examiner."

"Will do. I'll call the District Attorney tonight."

"Thanks," Farmer responded.

The chief left the scene to handle the reporters.

"Got anything?" Wilkes asked Sandra.

"No, all gone now in this weather," Sandra replied as the hard rain was now coming sideways at them. "Brent, what was the cause of death on Loretta Smith?"

"Loss of blood. All of the cuts were non-fatal, except one, the last one, he slit her throat."

"You may get something off this body, you should get her down as fast as you can with this weather."

"I agree. Do we have any idea who she is?"

"Yes, she's a prostitute out of Court Street in Jacksonville, same as Loretta Smith."

"Seems like we have a *perp* who's got something against prostitutes."

"What do you think of the crucifixions?"

"There have been quite a few serial killers in the United States, Sandra, dating back to the early 1900's. I've studied most of them, horrific, evil, heartless men, most of whom killed for sex or sadism or just because they enjoyed taking life, like Bundy. There are many people that don't understand that there are these guys walking around that are just evil. I don't get that feeling here, Sandra, I think this guy thinks he's doing God's work, but there is always one common thread."

"What's that?"

"They don't stop, until they're caught."

"Have you shared your thinking with Mac or Derrick?"

"It was too early, but now...do you know that Derrick's father is a preacher?"

"No I didn't, but I think you may be on the right track."

The medical examiner arrived, took pictures of the scene and assisted Wilkes and the others removing the body from the trees and placing her in a body bag. The group left the scene.

On the way out, Strong turned to Sandra, "Can we talk?"

"Sure. I came over with Mac, why don't you follow us back to my place. I can offer you some leftovers, hot coffee and privacy."

"Sounds good."

******

"Damn, Sandra, this chili is outstanding!" Farmer remarked as he took another spoonful out of the bowl in front of him.

"Try this crusty bread with it." Sandra placed a tray of warm bread and a plate of butter down in front of the two men who sat at her kitchen table.

"I'm starting to feel human again," Strong remarked as he sipped his coffee and sprinkled some grated cheese onto his chili, "Is this Mr. Coffee?"

"Yes, I thought, if it's good enough for 'Joltin' Joe' it's good enough for me." Sandra stood at the small counter that separated the kitchen from the living room. Her cat, Jerry, sat next to her on the counter. The three talked as they finished their late night meal.

Derrick pushed the bowl away and sipped his coffee from the mug Sandra had given him. "Why don't you tell us about Evelyn Martin?"

"Not much to tell," Sandra stood at the counter and lit a cigarette, "you said you needed a lead, so I made contact for you. You're right unpopular down there."

Strong looked at Farmer.

"Sandra, you said you'd let us know," Mac reminded her.

"And haven't I?" Sandra smiled.

"I guess we were thinking before you took any action."

"It's okay, Mac, we all make mistakes. Don't kick yourself in the ass over it." Another smile.

"I'm not kicking myself in the ass, Sandra, there's just some protocols that we need to agree on before you can work for us."

"Work for you? You're kidding, right? Been there, done that, Mac."

Farmer looked at Strong.

"So, what are you looking for, Sandra?" Strong asked.

"I'm looking for the bastard that killed my boys. I'll work with you, Derrick. This is going to explode tomorrow. This is small town south, they've never had anything like this before, it can get out of hand fast. The public needs to understand that you're working on leads and have persons of interest that you are investigating, they want to know you're making progress, otherwise you could have some real panic on your hands. Elected officials, like the sheriff and the DA, don't cotton too well to public outcry."

"Whoa Sandra, you think we can't handle the murder of two prostitutes from Jacksonville?"

"Think that through Derrick, what happens if he decides to crucify the next one in front of the Piggly Wiggly?"

The room went silent.

"Poison pellet?" Sandra asked.

"What?" Derrick answered.

"Scat!" Sandra chased Jerry off the counter, he jumped into his chair in the living room. She reached for a covered plate on the counter, removed the aluminum foil and revealed a dozen bite-size gingerbread cup cakes. She put them into her microwave, then opened the refrigerator, pulled out a tub of Cool Whip, removed the lid and placed it on the table between the two agents.

Ding!

Sandra opened the microwave door and the small kitchen was filled with the smell of gingerbread. She put the plate on the table next to the tub, "Just dip them guys, I'm not too fancy around here." Sandra grabbed one, dipped it into the Cool Whip and popped it into her mouth. As she chewed, some of the Cool Whip oozed out the side of her mouth, she wiped it away with her finger and then put her finger in her mouth and slowly sucked the Cool Whip off. The two men looked at her. She batted her eyelashes coyly at them. Both men laughed.

"More coffee, sirs?"

"If you're done with your presentation, absolutely," Derrick smiled.

"Thanks, Sandra, and even if you're not," Mac chuckled.

Sandra poured the coffee and set it in front of the two agents, who were working the poison pellets over pretty well. She returned to her coffee and cigarette on the counter.

"Why don't we start with what we've got, it might help you to prep for the press conference tomorrow, Derrick."

"Okay, two young women from Jacksonville have been viciously murdered in the past month. Both bodies were found in the Croatan. If we can find Dorothy Huggins' family we should release her name, age and hometown. Both women died of multiple stab wounds. No information on the crime scene during the investigation, can't deny or confirm."

"They'll probably ask about their disappearances, last seen where, time and day, and what they did for a living?" Sandra told him.

"We'll make that decision tomorrow with the DA," Derrick answered.

"Sandra, these will be tough times, especially around the holiday season, everyone is going to have to ride it out," Mac added.

"You guys are the professionals, I'm sure you'll do well. You might want to give some sort of warning or cautionary advice, in the public interest."

"Like what?" Mac asked.

"Keep out of the forest."

"It's hunting season, Sandra."

"Then at the least, you've warned them."

"Can we get back to Evelyn Martin?" Strong asked.

"That's a good idea," Sandra replied.

"Is she going to cooperate?"

"Damn, Derrick, you're not listening to me, I don't like that. Evey gave me the picture of Dorothy Huggins, don't you think that was cooperation."

"Evey?"

"I knew her when she worked in New York, we go back fifteen years. She trusts me."

"Will you ask her to come in and give us a statement?"

"Then she would not trust me."

"Does she want to see another woman killed?"

"Of course not. I talked to her last Friday the 5th. She told me that Dorothy disappeared Saturday night, November the 29th. Until then she thought Loretta Smith had run off, common in the business. Since last Friday, she's talked with her girls and she's installed security cameras. She knows we're looking for a big man and she's shared that with her girls. If you close her down, you'll never find this guy. I told her I'd liaison for her, she doesn't trust you guys. You remember the trust issue, don't you Derrick?"

"Yes."

"Good. If you want my help, it's my way, or the highway."

"I'm listening."

The tension in the room was growing.

"You don't need a statement, you need a motive and a connection. I gave you my theory on this guy's motive, I think there may be others who agree with that theory. I've dealt with my share of weirdoes, this guy fits like a glove. What we need here is the connection."

"You mean between Jacksonville and the Croatan," Strong responded.

Sandra smiled, "Exactly!"

Strong stood up and walked over to the opposite side of the counter. He looked down at Sandra. The feisty short woman with the big green eyes stared back at him with both courage and conviction.

"My father is a preacher, I consider myself a good Christian man. I may not have considered your—"

"I think we can eliminate your father from the suspects list," Sandra whispered gently.

Strong smiled and looked down at the counter, "May I?"

"Sure."

Strong took a cigarette out of Sandra's pack, he lit it and inhaled, blowing the smoke up over Sandra's head. "You're a smart woman, Sandra."

"But maybe just a bit bullheaded?" She asked.

"Maybe."

"Okay, if the war is over, can we talk about our biggest lead, and catching this bastard," Farmer asked. "We have two possibilities we've considered. First, he lives and works around Jacksonville where he picks them up and comes here to dump bodies. Second, he lives up here and goes to Jacksonville to pick them up, bring them up here and dump them in the forest."

"I'll take the second one, with variables," Sandra said as she walked around the counter and sat down in Strong's seat.

"Why?" Farmer asked.

"Because we think he knows me. I don't spend too much time in Jacksonville, he knows me from here."

"What are your variables, Sandra?" Farmer asked.

"He may not be a preacher, there's only a dozen of them in the area, it wouldn't take long to go measure their feet."

Mac laughed, "We've solved the case!"

"My point was, he could be a parishioner. Also, he might live or work in Jacksonville, but have a second place up here, like a hunting camp or family farm. We're looking for that trigger mechanism, what started this? Derrick, it's usually a change isn't it?"

"Yes, it could be a job change that took him to Jacksonville, something that exposed him to Evelyn's. If she tightened up things with her girls, we may be out of the woods for awhile, no pun intended."

"Evey's security may scare him off for awhile, but he's not going to stop until he's caught. What do we do?"

"We could try to lure him out," Farmer offered.

"How?" Sandra asked.

"He's not your biggest fan, Sandra," the SBI agent responded.

The room went silent, the only audible sound was the weather outside. Finally, Sandra spoke, "You want to use me as bait?"

"We could drop something at the press conference tomorrow, something about hiring a specialist to help track him down," Strong took another drag on his cigarette.

"Wouldn't he have to be there to hear that?" Sandra asked.

"No, if we present it right, the papers will pick it up. It's a story Sandra, that's how they work," Farmer answered.

"But we don't want you to get the feeling that your government manipulates the press," Strong butted the cigarette and smiled.

The Return of Sandra Love

The Party at the Post

Saturday, December 13th was a long day. The press conference in the afternoon had gone as well as could be expected. The District Attorney, Derrick Strong, Mac Farmer, Sheriff Baker, and Chief Briggs formed an imposing image as the DA shared what he could with the press and TV reporters. The names, ages and pictures of the two women were presented, along with cause of death. There were inferring questions from the press about the condition of the bodies, sourced from the couple that had found Dorothy Huggins, but no information about the crime scenes was released. A warning to the public regarding the forest was issued, a tip line phone number was given and the use of a local specialist assisting in the investigation was also shared. The conference was the lead story on the six o'clock news.

Sandra arrived at the VFW Post in Cedar Point a little after 7pm. The parking lot was full and there were some cars parked on both sides of VFW Road. Sandra drove past the post, turned around and parked on the opposite side of the road facing back toward Rte 58.

"Sandra!" Claire-Anne Bolt greeted her as she entered the large hall at the VFW Post. "Please join us at our table." Claire-Anne, her husband Fred, Ben Taylor and his wife Carolyn and a friend Anita Pointer were at the table. Claire-

Anne had reserved a seat for her friend between her and Ben Taylor.

"Thanks, Claire-Anne, good evening everyone," Sandra sat at the table.

The hall was filled with over a hundred people. A buffet was set up at the far end and some people were in line, while others mingled or waited at their table.

"Sandra, haven't seen much of you lately, missed you at the soup kitchen in Morehead City on Thanksgiving." Ben Taylor greeted her, "Been out of town?"

"Yes I was, Ben, visiting friends in Raleigh."

"Sandra makes friends easily, don't ya, hon?" Anita asked somewhat snidely.

Sandra never missed a beat, she looked across the round table and responded, "Yes I do Anita, it's a lost art, I'm sure you'd agree." Sandra gave her one of those kindergarten teacher smiles that drives everyone nuts. Anita backed off as Big Ben glared at her.

There were rumors around town that Big Ben and Anita had been having an affair for some time. Anita was a real estate agent who worked for Ben. She was a busty woman in her early thirties, who overdressed and spoke her mind, usually without a filter. As the rumor went, Ben Taylor had a hunting camp in the Croatan up Rte 58 that he used both in hunting season and on special occasions, out of season, but they were only rumors, no one in their right mind spoke about it publically.

"Will I see you at the kitchen on Christmas, Sandra?" Carolyn asked. Ben's wife was seated to his right and she leaned a bit into the table as she addressed her question.

"I may be out of town, Carolyn, but if I'm in town, I'll be there. I'll try and let you know as soon as I know for sure."

"Thank you. We enjoy your company on Christmas Day. You're a good little worker." The older woman added.

"Thank you, Carolyn."

"Well, who saw the news tonight?" Ben asked. "They found another body in the forest, this one was just off Star Hill Drive."

Sandra picked at her salad.

"I saw that, George was there. Looked like they had every agency in the area represented," Claire-Anne offered. "Sandra, are you helping them?"

"Sorry, Claire-Anne, I missed the news, help who, do what?"

"Helping this task force they're forming; catch this guy who's killing these girls and dumping them in the forest. George said you were there last night."

Sandra looked up from her salad and stared at Claire-Anne, "No, Claire-Anne, no one's asked me to help do anything with a task force."

"Sandra, everyone in the area knows that you know that forest better than the rangers," Big Ben remarked, "who would be better than The Bear Woman to help the police."

"The Bear Woman, who's that?"

"I thought you knew Sandra, that's what a lot of hunters call you."

"Really? How are they spelling that?"

 "B-E-A-R." Ben laughed. "Let's face it Sandra, you've taken more bear out of the Croatan in three years than I have in the last twenty."

"Well, that's the first time I've ever heard it. I'll take it as a compliment." Sandra raised her glass of water as if she was toasting, then she took a sip.

"I think it is intended that way," Ben replied.

The group talked for awhile about the recent event. Big Ben stated his concerns about the effect the murders might have on property values and tourism on the Crystal Coast, eventually, they made their way to the buffet. Sandra and Claire-Anne trailed behind Ben. The party was something Ben held every year for friends on the coast and often included vets from the Post and active military from Camp Lejeune.

"Good evening, Ben, this is quite the affair."

Sandra turned around, a pleasant looking, very tall man came up behind her.

"Thank you, John, Carolyn and I enjoy doing this each year."

Sandra stood between the two big men. Ben did the introduction, "Sandra, this is Reverend John Holly, he's our new pastor. John, this is a friend of mine, Sandra Horne, she lives in Peletier."

The tall lean man extended his hand, "John Holly, that's just a little L away from Holy."

Sandra smiled at the pun, "Nice to meet you, Pastor John, very clever."

"Thank you."

"John, you use that line on everyone you meet, and it always seems to work."

"Yes, it gives folks the impression that I'm smarter than I really am. Do you attend services, Sandra?"

"I was attending services at the Missionary Baptist Church in Peletier, but not recently. My husband and I divorced this year and I've been spending some one-on-one time with the Lord. I think he enjoys testing me."

"He seems to have his plans for all of us, doesn't he?"

"Yes, I've heard he works in mysterious ways."

"Well, if you ever feel you need some enlightenment, please feel free to call me or come to services, we Presbyterians welcome all."

"You can go with Fred and me anytime, Sandra," Claire-Anne added.

"Thank you, that's very kind."

The line at the buffet started with a huge pot of Jambalaya and was followed by shrimp, prime rib, ham, and Swedish meatballs. Sides included baked beans, scalloped potatoes, green beans, and grilled asparagus with sea salt. A punch made with orange juice, Seven-up, Hawaiian Punch and Raspberry sherbet awaited guests at the end of the line. The huge crystal bowl was surrounded by desserts.

"What a spread, Ben. You've out done yourself this year," Sandra remarked.

"Thanks Sandra, this is a bit of a balancing act isn't it?" Big Ben responded as he tried to hold his well-filled plate, a bowl of Jambalaya, and his cup of punch. "Guess we'll have to comeback for dessert."

Sandra took her bowl and plate to the table, then returned for her punch and dessert. They finished their meal as a DJ began to play music a little after 9pm. Ben and Carolyn Taylor got up to dance as Claire-Anne and Sandra chatted while Fred listened to Anita, at length.

"Hey, neighbor, how are you doing tonight?

Sandra looked up, "Hi, Mark, I didn't know you were coming tonight."

"This is my first Big Ben Taylor Christmas party, everyone's been talking about this for weeks. Now I see why."

"Sandra, introduce me," Claire-Anne whispered in her friend's ear.

"Mark, this is my best friend Claire-Anne Bolt, Claire-Anne this is Commander Mark Schneider, he is the new Director of Nursing at the base hospital and he owns the lot next to mine."

"A pleasure to meet you, Mark," Claire-Anne stood up as the sharp-dressed, well-built, handsome man in his late-thirties walked over and extended his hand. "How did you find our little soiree?"

"Nice to meet you, Claire-Anne. I met Ben when he came to the hospital back in July. We've been trying to develop some programs in the community for disabled vets. I transferred in from California in May, good to be back home."

"Would you like to join us?"

"Yes, thank you. Sandra, would you care to dance?"

"Sure."

The two walked onto the dance floor. Billy Joel's "It's Still Rock and Roll to Me" was playing. Sandra walked over to the DJ and spoke to him for a minute before returning to Mark.

"Everything okay?" He asked.

"Yes."

The song ended and the next song the DJ put on was Blondie's "Call Me." Sandra was wearing a beautiful long-sleeve, white cashmere sweater with a beaded front that showed off her figure well and went well with her green, black, and white patterned mid-knee skirt and black heels. As the music started, she reached down and grabbed the skirt in the middle and hiked it up over her knees. As she danced she tossed the skirt from side-to-side like a Flamenco dancer would. She slowly circled her dance partner who seemed transfixed on her body. Sandra seemed to be in a world of her own, then as Mark looked at her face, she smiled and winked at him. He started to laugh. The song ended and the two embraced and twirled for a moment.

Sandra whispered, "Just one more."

The next song was "You're the One That I Want," from the movie Grease. As the song started, Sandra lip-synced the words sung by

Olivia Newton-John to John Travolta. Mark was quick on the uptake and in one smooth motion pulled his black suit coat off and threw it across the floor. He wore a dress white tee-shirt underneath that showed off his barrel chest, muscular arms and tight waist. He lip-synced the Travolta words. The other dancers on the floor stopped dancing, backed away, and started shouting their approval as the couple skipped around the dance floor, posed, pointed at each other, and embraced as the song ended to a thunderous applause.

"I have got to go to the ladies room," Sandra told Mark as they walked off.

"That was great, a lot of fun. You dance very well. I'm going to hit the head too, see you back at the table."

Sandra wasn't in the stall for ten seconds when Claire-Anne burst through the door of the ladies room, "Sandra, where are you? Did you two plan that?" She shouted.

"No," Sandra reached for the roll.

"That was really great. Everyone is talking about it."

The toilet in the stall flushed and Sandra came out, she stepped over to the sink and washed her hands. As she used some paper towels to dry her hands she stepped in close to Claire-Anne and whispered, "Yes, I'm working with the task force. Don't mention it to anyone, it could cost me my life. Do you understand Claire-Anne?"

"Oh, hon, I'm sorry. Listen, you covered well. Let me know if you need any help, my lips are sealed."

"Thank you."

"Nice neighbor," Clair-Anne raised her right eyebrow.

"He's a nice guy. Come on, let's get back in there and party!"

The two returned to the table. Mark had pulled a chair up to the table between Sandra's and Ben's. Pastor John had taken Sandra's seat and was chatting with Mark, but stood and gave up the seat as the two women returned. There were fresh glasses of punch on the table and Big Ben stood up to propose a toast.

"To friends and family, Happy Holidays."

Sandra was thirsty from the dancing and gulped down the glass of punch and the soft, half-melted sherbet. She licked her lips. Something was wrong. She walked over to Ben, "Ben, is there any alcohol in this?"

"Two bottles of vodka, don't worry Sandra, with all the other mixers in there, one glass won't hurt you."

The Party at the Post

Sandra grabbed his arm and pulled him aside, "Ben, I'm an alcoholic. I've been dry for over three years."

"Sandra, I'm so sorry. I had no idea. Is there anything I can do?"

"No, you had no way of knowing, Ben. I need some water and some fresh air. Please excuse me."

Sandra left without a word. She pulled her green parka off the back of her chair and grabbed a glass of water at the bar on the way out. Outside in the parking lot she gulped all the water down and lit a cigarette. She looked up at the sky and the beautiful blanket of stars. "Help me with this one, please."

She walked around the parking lot and smoked another cigarette. As if an answer to her short prayer, she began to feel woozy. She walked back toward the door and stumbled. *One drink wouldn't do this to me,* she thought. Then her thinking stopped all together. She stumbled back to the parking lot, the road, and her truck. Between the parking lot and the street there was a twenty foot wide grass swale for water runoff. The swale had trees planted in it. She stepped off the lot, took a couple of steps down the swale and collapsed to the ground rolling to the bottom of the swale. She lay on her back, she looked Tree branches obliterated the sky. She tried to speak, nothing. Her face felt bloated, she went

to touch it, but her arm never moved. She felt
tired, she closed her eyes, and went out.

******

Sandra blinked her eyes. Something was
touching her face, it felt rough. She looked at it,
a late fall dandelion. She stared at it, it didn't
register. She heard voices, there were people in
the parking lot. Her mouth was open, but she
couldn't talk. She tried to get up, but her head
floated, it seemed she was detached from her
body. She felt sick to her stomach, then her
eyes rolled up in her head, and she went out
again.

The cool night air greeted Sandra as she swam
up from the depths of unconsciousness. She
had no idea where she was or how long she had
been unconscious. Something sticky and slimy
covered her breasts and hands. She lifted her
hands, they were covered with vomit. She had
no memory of being sick. She rolled over and
wiped her hand on the grass. The night was
absolutely still.

*M-must have drunk t-too much…c-can't
remember…need to go to bed….* Sandra
thought as she pulled her knees up and pushed
herself up onto all fours. She looked around.
She saw the front door light was on across the
parking lot at the post, but she didn't recognize
her location. She grabbed onto the trunk of the
tree she had been lying under and shimmied her
way up onto her feet. Slowly, she walked up the

swale and stepped into the parking lot, it was empty.

Thump!

Sandra collapsed onto her butt. She sat there trying to remember where she was and what was going on, but nothing registered. Then she noticed the big VFW sign on the building in front of her. *I must of fell off the wagon,* she thought as tears streamed out of her eyes, "I don't wanna live my life a drunk fool..." she mumbled as she fell over onto her side, groveled in the parking lot, and spit up more remnants of the dinner she couldn't recall. She lay there for a few minutes crying, then she got mad.

"Be strong, Sandra! Be strong! Be strong!" Again and again she repeated the phrase that she lived her life by; she found herself standing up straight. She looked at the sign again, "VFW eh... Michael probably left me here. Fuck you dickhead, I'll walk home!"

She turned around and again started toward the road, angry that her husband would abandon her like this. She swayed back and forth as she walked unintentionally to the lot's exit. She looked across the street and there was her truck. "Ah, he left it for me. He's such a sweetie."

Sandra climbed into the truck and fumbled for her keys in her coat pocket. She pulled them they were sticky and slimy. She cleaned them off on her skirt. She looked at her skirt, she remembered, she and Michael were

divorced. She looked at the skirt again, she
couldn't remember the party, but she
remembered there was a party, maybe that was
why she was there. She turned the engine and
lights on and looked at the clock in the truck, it
read 4:15. She put the truck in gear and it
lurched forward.

Easy now, Sandra thought as she drove down
VFW Road to the stop sign at Rte 58. Sandra
stopped at the intersection of Rte 58. No lights in
either direction. She pulled out onto the highway
and headed toward Peletier. As she drove two
headlights appeared in her rearview mirror.

Wait a minute, she thought, *this could be the
killer.* She stared into the mirror, her eyes
transfixed on the two headlights.

BAM! BAM! BAM!

Sandra jumped, startled by the noise. She
refocused on the road just as the front of her
truck hit the fourth mailbox. *BAM!*

Sandra swerved back onto the road as the blue
flashing light came on behind her and she heard
the police siren. She pulled her truck over to the
side of the road and turned off the engine.

The officer pulled in behind her and got out of
his car. He walked up to the truck and pointed
his flashlight inside. Sandra was slumped over
on the front seat, out like a light!

******

"She's in the back."

Mack Farmer followed Chief Briggs back to a small room in the back of the Cape Carteret police station. Sandra sat on a chair with her head resting on her hands on the desk in front of her. She was asleep.

Farmer moved her shoulder and roused her. "Sandra, Sandra, come on Sandra, wake up."

Sandra stirred and lifted her head up off the desk. "Mac...what are you doing here? Where am I?"

"I've come to get you. Do you know what happened?"

"I c-can't remember...was I drinking?"

"No, hon, we think you've been drugged. You blew a .01 for the officer who brought you in; he said you were impaired, we need to find out from what."

Sandra shook her head and stood up. "Y-yes...someone must have slipped me a *Mickey* last night."

"George said they brought you in after you ran over some mailboxes on Rte 58 early this morning. Were you at Ben Taylor's party last night?"

"Yes, I went, but I don't remember much. I think Claire-Anne was there, what's that horrible smell?"

"That's you, Sandra. No alcohol, you must have vomited after you were drugged."

"Can you get me out of here, Mac?"

"Given the circumstances, George will let me take you up to the hospital to draw blood. I've called to get the lab analysis *stat*."

"What's stat?"

Farmer smiled, "It's Latin for immediately."

"What time is it?"

"It's a little after 10am."

"What day is it?"

"Sunday, December 14...1980."

"Let me go home and get out of these clothes first."

"Sure."

The two drove over to Sandra's, she fed Jerry, showered, and changed clothes. They drove up to the Carteret Hospital in Morehead City and had blood and urine samples taken. The lab results showed no alcohol, but tested positive for Rohypnol. Rohypnol or *roofies* in the drug community, was a Benzodiazepine that was used as an hypnotic, sedative, anticonvulsant, skeletal muscle relaxant and was better known to the public as a date rape drug. Used with alcohol, the adverse effects of the drug are synergized and can cause toxicity and death.

"You dodged a bullet on this one, Sandra," Mac's voice had an edge to it as he drove down Rte 70 and turned onto Rte 24. "Do you have any idea who might have done this?"

"Mac, I don't remember much of last night. Let's go see Claire-Anne. She should be home from church by now. What time is it?"

"It's just after 3pm. I don't think you're a hundred percent yet. Strong sees his dad on Sundays, we could see her tomorrow, all of us."

"I'll be fine, Mac. I need a good night's sleep, a jog in the forest, and a couple of hours in the gym tomorrow, but I want to know what happened last night, now. You good to go?"

"You bet."

The Return of Sandra Love

On The Trail

Farmer drove down to Claire-Anne's. She lived on Yaupon Drive, in Cape Carteret, a block from Bogue Sound. Claire-Anne answered the door, Fred was watching football.

"Sandra, Mac, come on in. Where did you go last night? You didn't even say good-bye."

"Long story, Claire Anne. We need you to fill in some gaps," the two stepped inside.

Claire-Anne read the look of concern on her friend's face, "Fred's watching the game, come on in the kitchen, we'll talk."

The two filled her in on what had happened and asked her to recount the evening as she remembered it. "Pretend Sandra has no memory of anything last night," Mac started, "because, she doesn't. Be specific and as detailed as you can, particularly with anyone she spoke to or inter-acted with; we think whoever did this might be our guy."

Claire-Anne was visibly upset and eager to help. Her years as a magistrate had given her plenty of practice with testimony. She recounted the evening's events as she remembered them. Mac took notes as she explained who was sitting at the table, the buffet line, Sandra's dancing with Mark, Big Ben's toast and Sandra's sudden exit.

"I haven't danced in years," Sandra commented.

"You even got Pastor John's attention, Sandra, he said you were an excellent dancer. That you had probably been a dancer at one time. You and Mark were dancing to that song from Grease, 'You're the One That I Want.' "

Bingo! Sandra thought. "Who's Pastor John?" She asked.

"Oh, hon, you were out of it, weren't you. You met him last night in the buffet line, he invited you to services and he was at our table while you were dancing."

Sandra looked at Farmer.

"So while I was putting on this exhibition with Mark, the pastor came to our table?"

"Yes he sat...HOLY SHIT! You think Pastor John is a serial killer? Are you nuts? What did that drug do to your brain, Sandra?"

"We don't think anything, Claire-Anne. We're just trying to put this thing together. We don't want to see anyone else murdered. When this pastor came to your table, where did he sit?" Mac asked.

"He sat in Sandra's seat. We talked and watched Sandra and Mark dance. I was right there all the time, he couldn't have put anything in her drink, I would have seen it."

"He couldn't have because you were there with him?"

"Yes."

"Watching Sandra?"

Claire-Anne was quiet, she realized she couldn't have watched the pastor and the dancing at the same time. And she knew she had watched the dancing!

"After the dance was over, did Sandra come back to the table?"

"Oh my God! Mac, you're right. Sandra went into the ladies room and I got up and followed her in. I wanted to tell Sandra that her dancing was great."

"How long were you gone?"

"Long enough! That's when he did it."

"Claire-Anne, help me out here. No one did anything yet, if we assume, we make an *ass* out of *u* and *me*. Let's just stay with the facts. Earlier, you said Big Ben made a toast, what did you drink?"

"When Sandra and I came out of the ladies room we went straight to the table. Everyone had a fresh glass of punch. I thought Ben got them for the toast."

"Probably, we'll check that. Anything else?"

"No. Sandra got up and left."

Mac thanked Claire-Anne and reminded her of the importance of secrecy while the investigation continued. Then the two left.

On the way to Sandra's Mac asked, "What do you think?"

"I have a short list, but I don't want to jump across the Grand Canyon on this. He might have been taking a run at me, I'll give you that, but maybe we just have some *perv* who likes the way I dance and hasn't been laid in the last ten years. We have some suspects with means and opportunity, but still no motive. "

"Who's on your short list?"

I'd start with Pastor John, then my neighbor Mark and then there's Ben Taylor. You and Derrick have some work to do, bring them in, rough them up and measure their feet." Sandra smiled.

"Funny," Mac replied, "Listen, I know your theory about this guy, you see him as mission-oriented, I think you may be right, but I can tell you that with serial killers if motive is not sexual, it usually goes unidentified. Brent thinks there are some guys that are just born evil."

"I need a day off, why don't we meet Tuesday at your office, 10am?"

On the Trail

"Sounds good. I want to talk to Ben Taylor tomorrow."

They picked up Sandra's truck on the side of Rte 58 and drove up to her lot.

"I'll walk you back," Mac said as he opened his door and walked around the car.

"Who's going to walk you out? It's getting dark."

Mac unbuttoned his coat, "My two friends, Mr. Smith and Mr. Wesson." He parted his coat and Sandra saw Mac's holstered .357 S&W mag.

"Good company."

******

Sandra sat at her kitchen table as she strapped the ankle-holster with her Beretta .25 semi-automatic around her calf. She pushed her sweat pants down and finished her coffee. She put her hoodie on over her tee-shirt and zipped it up. She stepped out of her trailer, locked the front door and started jogging down the path behind her trailer toward Mark Schneider's lot.

Mark's cabin was almost new. He had bought it from a Marine who transferred to the west coast earlier in the year when he was transferred to Camp Lejeune. It was almost a mile from her trailer. Sandra started out slow, but as she got to Mark's property line she was feeling stronger. No fitful sleep last night. She had gone to bed around 9pm and slept straight through to 6am.

The cool Monday morning air revived her and she needed the exercise. She could see the back of the cabin as she approached and the lane in front that came in from Peletier Loop Road. There was no vehicle in front of the cabin. She jogged up into the back yard and then around to the screened-in front porch. She opened the screen door and stepped inside. She knocked on the front door, no answer. She knocked again, nothing. Sandra tested the door knob, it was locked.

She took a quick look around and then pulled two paper clips from her pocket. She straightened the clips out and slid the first one into the key hole until it stopped. She slid the second one in under the first until it would go no further, then she pushed in hard, the lock opened. She stepped into the cabin and closed the door. The cabin had a great room with a fireplace on the far right. The room fed into the kitchen on the left, between the rooms was a short hallway that led back to two bedrooms separated by a shared bathroom.

Sandra looked around the living room. There was unopened mail from the Navy on an end table addressed to Mark. She walked out to the kitchen. There were dirty dishes in the sink, but nothing unusual. She headed to the bedrooms. The one on the left had an unmade bed. She stepped in and looked around. The December 1980 issue of Playboy was on the nightstand, under the stand were a stack of Playboy magazines. Sandra smiled, everything looked normal. She walked over to the closet and stooped down. There were several pairs of shoes and boots on the floor. She looked in a pair of dress shoes, they were marked 10EE. She looked in a pair of boots and a pair of sneakers, all were marked 10W. She stepped toward the door that lead to the bathroom. Sandra turned suddenly, she heard a vehicle outside coming up the lane.

She headed toward the front door. She could see Mark pulling up into the front yard, "Shit!" She gasped. Her mind raced. "Think, Sandra, think!"

She turned toward the back door of the cabin, then she turned back and quickly locked the front door. She ran across the room and started to open the back sliding door, it wouldn't budge. She could hear the car door outside slam shut. She looked at the lock, it was open. She pushed again, it wouldn't move. She looked down and a piece of shim wood was in the track preventing the door from moving. Sandra realized if she removed the wood, she couldn't exit the house and replace it. Mark would know that someone had been in the cabin; she didn't want him on guard. She heard the front porch screen door slam close. He was on the porch! She could hear him setting grocery bags down on the porch. She turned, and moved silently across the room and down the hall. She looked at the two bedroom entrances as the front door opened. She stepped quietly into the spare bedroom. It had a double bed, a single nightstand with a small lamp and nothing else. She crept around the bed and lay down on the floor between the bed and the far wall. She tried to slide under the bed, but the frame was just a few inches off the floor, no way. She could hear Mark in the kitchen.

Holy shit! She thought. *It's been almost ten years since I was shot in Freddie's trailer, I haven't learned a God Damn thing.* Then she realized her pistol was strapped around her right leg. Slowly, she reached down, lifted her pant leg and pulled the gun out. She placed it on her stomach as she listened to the cupboard doors opening and closing in the kitchen.

She could hear Mark's footsteps as he walked down the hall, she slid her right foot under the bed frame and squeezed her right shoulder against the bed. Mark stepped into the room and walked to the closet at the foot of the bed, he was no more than six feet away. He was carrying a grocery bag in his left arm that partially blocked his view. He opened the closet door and bent over placing the bag on the floor of the closet.

She couldn't help herself, *Nice ass,* she thought.

Mark ripped open a pack of toilet paper and removed a roll. He closed the closet door, turned to his right and entered the bathroom through the door from the spare bedroom. Sandra could hear the toilet seat drop as Mark sat down on the throne. A moment later she heard him go and the toilet flush. Then she heard the tub faucet turn on and the heavy sound of water hitting the tub floor. In a few moments the shower came on and she heard the sound of the shower curtain closing, she took a deep breath and slowly raised her head. Mark was showering and singing, "You're the One That I Want." His singing was terrible.

Sandra extricated herself from behind the bed. She crept out of the room and down the hall. She tried the front door, it was unlocked. She stepped out onto the front porch, returned the gun to the ankle holster, turned around and knocked on the front door. No response.

"Mark, you in there!" She shouted.

"Who's there?" He shouted back. The shower water stopped.

"It's your neighbor, Sandra. Should I come back?"

"Hell no! I'm in the shower, come on in. I'll be out in a couple of minutes. Grab some coffee, on the counter."

Sandra smiled. Her little ruse had worked. She found coffee mugs in one of the cupboards and poured a cup from the pot on the Mr. Coffee machine. She poured some sugar into the coffee from a glass container that you normally find in diners. Then she started to open some drawers looking for a spoon.

"The one next to the dishwasher."

She turned around and Mark stood at the end of the hall toweling off his hair. He was dressed in a pair of navy blue sweat pants and was bare-chested.

Sandra reached in the drawer and pulled out a spoon. She stirred her coffee and looked at the handsome, well built man. He reminded her of her Jake in Newport, but older and with shorter hair.

"I wanted to come over and talk to you. I owe you an apology for my sudden disappearance Saturday night."

"I was wondering what happened to you. Was it something I said?" Mark smiled.

"I didn't know there was vodka in the punch. I'm an alcoholic, dry for three years. I was a little upset when I found out. I have to avoid temptation, so I left."

"Well, we were worried about you. Guess you got home alright."

"What time did you leave?" Sandra sat down at the table, sipped her coffee and acted as though the question was simply filler.

"Not long after you left. Anita came over."

"Oh really? And how did that go?"

"Well, let's just say that woman can talk. Let me get a shirt on. Can you stay for a few minutes?"

"Sure."

Mark walked back to the bedroom and returned in a few minutes with a tight fitting tee-shirt on and his short hair combed.

"I had a great time with you, especially the dancing," he said.

"Yes, I heard we were a hit."

"Yes, even that Pastor Holly remarked about us."

"Sorry I missed that. What did he say?"

"He said you were a very good dancer and he thought that maybe you had danced professionally."

"No such luck. Anything else?"

"No, but..."

"But what?"

"Well, remember that toast Ben Taylor made."

"*Hmm-hum...*"

"When you drank, he was...ahhh..." Mark hesitated.

"Ahhh... what?"

"He was...ah...looking at your chest." Mark looked uncomfortable.

"How do you know?"

"Ah...okay, let me rephrase. Pastor Holly and me may have glanced at your chest."

"Men."

"Hey Sandra, we're designed that way."

"Was Pastor Holly still there when you and Anita left?"

"Funny you should ask that. He left right after you did. He said he hadn't finished his Sunday sermon. He seems like a really nice guy, don't you think?"

"I really didn't get much time with him. He did invite me to services, I'll make it a point to talk to him."

"Speaking about talking, I have to go out this morning, but if you'd like, why don't you have dinner with me sometime?"

"That sounds nice. I'm seeing someone in Raleigh right now, why don't we make it a breakfast or lunch. How's your work schedule look?"

"I'm working four twelve's right now. Just got off actually."

"What do you mean, twelve's?" Sandra played dumb so she could confirm Mark's exact schedule.

"Twelve hour shifts four days a week, 7pm to 7am."

"So you work Sunday night through Thursday morning, that's great. You really have a four day weekend, from Thursday morning until Sunday night."

"Oh how I wish. I work every other weekend. It's just part of the job."

"How about family?"

"My wife and thirteen year old son are in San Diego, we divorced about two years ago. She has full custody, but I have visits and try to keep in touch. Transferring here makes it tough."

"I know about that keeping in touch thing, believe me," Sandra responded as her son Tony came to mind.

"I need to finish some Christmas shopping this week. How's next week sound?" Mark asked.

"I may be going to Raleigh this weekend for a week or so. Let's play it by ear, don't worry, we'll get together."

Sandra finished her coffee and said good-bye. She jogged back down the path to her trailer.

******

The Return of Sandra Love

Sandra got back to her trailer, showered and dressed. She threw her Saturday night clothes in the truck, she dropped them at the dry-cleaners on her way. She drove her truck over to the Presbyterian Church. Sandra walked into the office.

"Good morning, my name is Sandra Horne, is Pastor John in today?"

"He's out right now, but I expect him back in the next ten minutes or so. Would you like to wait for him?" The volunteer greeter asked.

"Yes, I can wait a few minutes, uh..."

"Lisa, Lisa Farnsworth. Can I get you something to drink, a coffee or tea?"

"Yes, coffee, thank you."

"How do you take yours?"

"Black with two sugars, please."

"I'll be right back." Lisa started to get up to go into a small room off to the side behind her desk.

"Can I help?"

"Sure, come on back."

The two walked back into what looked like a small break room. It had a card table and four chairs, a refrigerator and a counter with cupboards. There was a small sofa on the back wall, under a window. Sandra's eye caught a coat rack and umbrella stand in the far corner, under it was a pair of rubber galoshes.

"I saw you at Big Ben's party Saturday night. You sure can dance, Miss Horne."

"Please call me Sandra."

"That fella you were dancing with, do you know him?"

"Mark Schneider, Commander Schneider, I should say. Yes, he's a nurse who works on base and he's also my neighbor."

"Well, we enjoyed watching the two of you dance, quite entertaining."

"Speaking about dancing, my feet have been bothering me lately, if you don't mind..." Sandra walked over to the sofa and sat down. She removed one of her boots and pretentiously rubbed her foot. Lisa brought the coffee over and placed it on the coffee table in front of the sofa.

"You don't see those around too much anymore," Sandra leaned over and picked up one of the rubber boots.

"They're Pastor John's. He keeps them here for bad weather." Lisa then whispered, "You're right, Sandra, I'm afraid our new pastor may be a bit old fashioned." She giggled.

Sandra turned the boot over, "It's huge, he must have big feet."

"Look inside, maybe it says how big—"

"Size thirteen," Sandra read the stamped number inside the boot, "that's pretty big."

"Lisa!" Pastor John had returned and called out for Sandra's companion.

"In here, Pastor John." She turned to Sandra and whispered, "Better put it back."

"Okay," Sandra whispered back, as if the two were sharing top secret information. She returned the boot and slipped her own back on as the pastor entered the break room.

"Hi, how are you doing? Sandra isn't it?" The tall 6'5" pastor walked over to the sofa.

"Yes, Sandra Horne, I thought I would drop by and see if you have some time when we could meet and talk. I'm starting to think the Lord is giving me the run around."

Pastor John smiled, "He's been known to do that every once in a while, I just think of it as *free will*. We're pretty busy this time of year, come on back to my office and we'll get something on my calendar."

"That sounds good. I might be out of town next week. Maybe after the first." Sandra stood up, she came up to Pastor John's shoulder. "Lisa, thanks for the coffee. Hope to see you soon, have a Merry Christmas."

"You too, Sandra."

The two walked back to the pastor's office.

"Please have a seat, Sandra." Pastor John sat down, reached under the calendar on the desk in front of him and pulled out a new 1981 Week-at-a-Glance planner. "How's Monday, January 5th, sound."

"Great. What time?"

"How's 11am?"

"Perfect."

"Do you know what you want to talk about?"

Sandra's eyes narrowed, "Good and evil."

"Guess I should bone up on those two." Pastor John smiled.

Sandra didn't. She stared at him for a few seconds. He looked back uncomfortably, but couldn't hold his eyes on her. He reached for a pen and wrote the appointment in his planner. When he was finished, he looked up, Sandra held her gaze. Then, out of the blue, "Did you have fun Saturday night, Pastor John?"

"Yes I did. What a kind man Ben Taylor is to do that each year for friends and family. How about you?"

"I must have had something that disagreed with me, I had to leave early."

"Yes, you seemed to be in a hurry. Feeling better now?"

"Yes, thanks. Did you stay late?"

"Actually, I left shortly after you, hadn't finished my Sunday sermon. Everyone enjoyed your dancing. Did you ever dance professionally?"

"No, can't say that I have, but when I was younger I had some friends who were professional dancers, I may have picked up some moves from them."

"Well, you dance well. It was fun to watch you."

"Thank you, Pastor John. I'm looking forward to our next meeting." Sandra stood up and extended her hand across the desk. Pastor John reached out and grasped her hand. Sandra gripped him hard, but his hand was so large that it seemed to have little effect on him. Sandra smiled at him and said, "Now don't do anything crazy this holiday, we already have one crazy running around here." She released her grip, but before she could withdraw her hand, he gripped her hand and held it firmly.

"Yes, we do. Okay, nothing crazy until I see you again. Merry Christmas, Sandra." He released her hand.

"Merry Christmas, Pastor John."

Puzzle Pieces

"Hi, Jenny, it's Sandra. How have you been?"

"Worried, haven't heard from you in awhile, everything okay down there?"

"Well, I'm having an adventure here on the coast, but don't do any worrying, I'm fine."

"The press conference made the news up here. Sounds like you've got a real *nutcase* running around down there. Sandra, I'm not just asking for myself, Lane and Sara were worried too. Is this adventure going to interfere with your coming up for Christmas? Sara is out of school this Friday and Lane has a list of plans for all of us for the holiday."

"Any wild horses up there?"

"I've got them all corralled."

"Then there's nothing that could keep me away. I've got to do some Christmas shopping, any requests?" Sandra asked.

"You're on your own, Sandra. What do you get for people like Lane and Sara?"

"Real estate?"

"Funny. I think the right answer is, you."

"That's kind of you, Jenny," Sandra paused for a moment. "Listen, Jenny, I need you to send me something in the mail tomorrow." Sandra explained her idea, based on Jenny's inadvertent suggestion.

"That's a great idea, Sandra. I'll take care of that right away."

"Thanks, Jenny. How's Friday afternoon sound?"

"I'll leave a light on for you, now can you get me back in the loop."

Sandra filled Jenny in on the events of the last ten days, including the party at the post. She told her she was meeting with Farmer and Strong the next day. Jenny was worried about Sandra's safety and advised her to be on her toes. Sandra promised her that she would be careful. Then Jenny filled Sandra in on life in the fast Lane. Sandra laughed at the pun. Jenny told Sandra that all of them had a wonderful Thanksgiving and were looking forward to seeing her. She finished with, "Sandra, you have really made a wonderful impact on our family."

"Thanks, Jenny, the feeling is reciprocal. See you all on Friday."

Monday night Sandra sat on one of the stumps to the left of her trailer. A hand-built rock fire ring in front of her contained a crackling fire of red oak logs she had taken that summer. Sandra often sat out in front of her trailer at night, it reminded her of the year she had spent in the

Puzzle Pieces

Great Smokey Mountains in Tennessee. She allowed herself these moments and often thought about what her life would have been like with Robert Allen or what had become of her Jake and her friend Billy Arrowood. Sometimes she talked to the Lord over coffee and a smoke, she thought of him as good company, a friend. She always started by thanking him for everything she had in her life, but on occasion she'd ask him for the wisdom or strength to survive an ordeal or just live a good life. She often apologized for her earlier life and the things she had done, she wanted to please him.

Tonight's discussion was about Zack and Cooper.

"Good evening, Lord, it's me Sandra. I won't take much of your time tonight, I know how busy you must be this time of the year. I hope you're taking good care of my boys, please tell them how much I love and miss them." She took a sip of coffee and pulled a pack of cigarettes out of her pocket and lit one, her hand was shaking. She blew the smoke up into the cool night air and watched it as it disappeared into the dark. Her eyes moistened. "They like kisses, please give them some for me tonight. Tell them they're from Mommy." The tears rolled out of her big green eyes and down her cheeks as her lips quivered; she tried to steel herself from the pain. "I can't be strong all the time, Lord, I don't have your strength." She blubbered.

Sandra wiped her eyes and nose on her shirt sleeve. "So how was your day?" She smiled and wiped her face again. She took another drag on her cigarette. "If we're made in your image, do you ever cry?" She asked as she smoked. "Guess you must have some days that are better than others. Do you feel heartbreak when we let you down?" She chatted on for a few minutes, ending with, "Listen, if you ever feel you need someone to talk to, feel free to give me a call. Love you." Then she finished with the Lord's Prayer. She stayed in front of the fire until it died down to embers, then she went to bed.

******

"I heard about the party, Sandra, it's time we did something about this son of a bitch," Derrick Strong commented as he and Farmer entered the conference room at the SBI office in Jacksonville and sat down.

"Fill me in on what you've got, did you talk to Ben Taylor yet?" Sandra asked.

"Yes, yesterday, at his office. He told us that he and Pastor John had brought the punch to the table. Sandra, he was hosting the party, why would he spike your drink, he was there with his wife and stayed until mid-night. He's out. That leaves us Mark Schneider and John Holly."

"Derrick, you're FBI, don't you have jurisdiction on base?"

"I'll have to go through NIS."

"NIS?"

"Naval Investigative Service. Shouldn't be a problem, but I would need to clear through them first. What's up?"

"I spent some time with Mark yesterday morning. Got a good look around his cabin, I think we're barking up the wrong tree with him."

"We were going to take a look at his access to ether on base."

"He wears a size 10 shoe."

"Sounds like you had a good look around, Sandra," Mac commented.

"Don't get too excited, Mac, he wasn't there. Derrick, you need to check his work schedule, he told me he works four twelve's and every other weekend, 7pm to 7am. Let's see when he was working and when he was off, he had to have had opportunity right?"

Strong nodded.

"If you're working that, I'll see what I can get out of Pastor Holly," Mac suggested.

"You mean Pastor Big Foot don't you?"

"What do you mean, Sandra?"

"He wears a size 13 boot."

"How the hell do you know that?" Farmer asked, "I thought you just met him."

"Since Claire-Anne told us Sunday afternoon that he invited me to attend services, I stopped by his church yesterday. There's a pair of galoshes, old, but nice for walking in bogs and marshes, in the break room where I had coffee with the volunteer greeter. She told me that they belong to Pastor John, says he keeps them there for rainy days, they're size 13."

"I'll be damned." Strong whispered.

"And I thought you were just a pretty face," Farmer reached out and patted Sandra on the back, "nice work."

"Hang on guys, all the puzzle pieces don't fit yet."

"What do you mean?" Strong asked.

"I never met this guy before in my life. I thought we agreed that whoever did this, knows me, knows where I live."

"Maybe the pastor knew you, but you didn't know him. Maybe he's been tailing you, maybe he's a stalker type," Mac offered.

"Maybe won't cut it. We have to prove it," Strong continued, "we need to figure out how to get after him. Mac, can you run a complete background on this guy? I'll get after Commander Schneider's info."

"And I'll go to Raleigh for Christmas, you have the number." Sandra stood up, "But first I'm going to do a little shopping and see what's doing with Evelyn Martin. By the way, I picked up a little Christmas present for you two. You can work on it while I'm gone." Sandra reached into her purse and placed the present on the conference table.

"What's that?" Strong asked.

"It's called a Rubik's Cube. It's a lot like this case, you have to put it all together." Sandra walked toward the door.

"What about Holly?" Farmer asked.

"Oh, didn't I tell you, I have an appointment with him, January 5th at 11am." Sandra opened the door.

"Sandra, you could screw this thing up if you're not careful, what are you going to talk to him about?" Strong asked.

"Good and evil." Sandra winked at them and left.

******

Evelyn Martin walked into Luigi's and looked back at her table. Someone was seated there facing the back of the restaurant. She walked back. Sandra was seated, waiting.

"Didn't recognize you at first, you always had a lot of looks, Sandra."

The Return of Sandra Love

"I'm business casual today."

"Well, this is a pleasant surprise," The older woman sat down across from her friend.

"How's it going, Evey?"

"Business is off a bit, but that comes with this time of year. Some of my customers actually feel they should spend time with family at Christmas. I don't get it?"

Sandra smiled.

"You'll like this though, I've introduced gift cards for my clients."

"NO!" Sandra shouted and then put her hand over her mouth and started to laugh.

"And I give a few out to the palms I have to cross here in Jacksonville. It's a free one, they love them."

"You are too much, Evey," Sandra giggled.

"I try and plan some events for the girls, shopping or parties, something to help them through what can be the saddest time of the year."

"I remember."

"I saw the press conference on the news, thanks for limiting their background to, 'they both worked in Jacksonville.' "

Puzzle Pieces

Their waiter approached the table. "Tony, one tab here today."

"Yes, Miss Evelyn. Are you ready to order?"

"What's the special today?"

"Louie's lasagna."

"Sandra, you need to try this, it has cheese in it from here to Denmark."

Sandra nodded, "Sounds good, and a water."

Evelyn ordered a glass of wine, Tony took the menus and left.

Sandra lit a cigarette and asked, "How are your girls doing with this?"

"I met with them as we discussed, we talked about 'stranger danger'; they're more comfortable now with the security cams and my guys walk them to their cars, no exceptions. Some of them have pepper spray. How are things going at your end?"

"I attended a party Saturday night at the VFW in Cedar Point. One of the big shots on the coast throws it every year. Someone slipped a *roofie* into my punch, we think he was making a run at me."

"Jesus, Sandra, you need to be careful."

"Thanks, Evey, I will be. I think we have a short list as a result of the party, and I have a prime suspect based on something I stumbled across yesterday. I have a description of this guy, here." Sandra took a piece of paper out of her purse, it had a detailed description of John Holly on it, she handed it to Evelyn. "Be sure your girls and your security guys see this."

"Thanks, Sandra. Excellent Christmas present, very thoughtful."

Tony served their lunch. The lasagna was outstanding. They finished their meal and walked out of the Italian restaurant.

"Merry Christmas, hon," Evelyn hugged Sandra.

"You too, Evey. I'll be in Raleigh for a week or so, leaving Friday. Be careful."

The women parted.

The man sat in his car in a parking lot across the street, watching.

"Fucking whore, you just don't listen, do you?"

******

Tuesday night Sandra sat in front of her fire ring, she was making S'mors for dessert. After melting her marshmallows she transferred them from her stick to the chocolate covered graham cracker and gave Jerry a piece. The cat took the S'mor, walked away from the fire ring and lay down. He licked the marshmallow over and over again savoring its sweetness.

Puzzle Pieces

"Still got that sweet tooth, eh?" She asked. The cat looked up at her, he had licked the small amount of marshmallow off the cracker. He began to play with the cracker as if it were a toy. "We're going away for Christmas this year. We're going to see Sara, would you like that pal?" Jerry was too busy playing with his cracker to pay any attention. Sandra's attention turned toward the forest. She pushed her Cubs baseball hat back on her head and listened. After a few minutes went by she noticed, no rhythm.

"He's out there," she whispered to Jerry, "I can feel the son of a bitch, watching."

The cat seemed to sense Sandra's change of tone. He got up and walked over to Sandra. He jumped up into her lap and turned as if he was thinking, *We'll take him on together.* Sandra picked up her cat. "Not here, Jerry," she whispered.

She stood up and walked into her trailer.

He moved.

He moved without a sound, from behind the tree at the top of the far ridge to another tree in the same sight line halfway to Sandra's bridge. He raised his binoculars and focused them on the trailer. He could see Sandra through the thin curtain as she walked around in the kitchen. Slowly, he moved down the path to the bridge. The trailer was now out of site. He knew he couldn't be seen now, but he maintained his

183

stealth as he crept his way down the hill, across the bridge and up the path until he could see the trailer again. He knew the importance of stealth in the forest.

He peered out from the tree he had moved behind. Sandra's silhouetted head, shoulders and ball cap could be seen on the curtains as she sat at the kitchen table. Slowly, he slid the strap of the rifle off his shoulder and raised the weapon toward the window. He looked into the scope, the crosshairs on the window. He rested the rifle against the tree to steady his aim. He moved the crosshairs until they rested on Sandra's silhouetted head.

Click! He pressed the safety off and took a long slow breath. Then he applied pressure to the rifle's trigger.

KAPOW!

The rifle's report echoed through the woods as the bullet flew the seventy five yards to the trailer and crashed through the window. He quickly refocused his sight through the scope, the silhouette was gone.

"And that's how it's done bitch," he murmured as he stepped out from behind the tree.

BAM! BAM! BAM!

The first bullet caught him square in the chest. The impact knocked him backwards and the rifle dropped from his hand. He fell on his back, stunned. The next shot flew over his head close enough that he heard it whistle by. The third bullet hit the tree he had stood behind and bark from the tree flew down hitting him in the head and shoulder. He rolled over, grabbed his rifle and looked up to his right. The forest was dark and silent.

BAM! BAM! BAM!

He saw the orange and yellow flames flash out of the end of the gun barrel as he peered into the blackness. The bullets hit the ground where he had fallen. He could hear the footsteps as the shooter ran through the woods toward him. He jumped to his feet, turned and ran. He was across the bridge and half way up the hill when the shooter stepped onto the path and raised the pistol. Then he jumped off the path and into the woods.

"Come on back you bastard, let's dance! Come back anytime, I'll be waiting for you!" Sandra shouted into the dark. Despite her rapid breathing, she could hear his footsteps fade as he ran through the underbrush. She knew he would not return, for the same reason she would not follow. In the forest, the victor is always the one who lies in wait.

She released the hammer on her Colt .45. As she walked up the path to her trailer, she thought, *The first shot knocked him down, I'll check for blood in the morning.*

When she got to the trailer, she walked behind it and entered through the back door she had exited from a short while ago. She stepped up into the kitchen, her full-head wig mannequin lay shattered on the floor. There was a hole in her front window and a hole in the back wall of the trailer just above the range. Jerry was curled up in his chair as if nothing had happened.

"Time to go to bed, pal." She turned the lights off and walked back to her bedroom. She dropped the clip out of her gun and inserted the second clip she carried in her jacket. She put the gun on the nightstand, took off her clothes and got in bed. Jerry jumped up on the bed as Sandra turned off the lamp beside her bed. Jerry purred as Sandra's mind raced.

******

Wednesday morning found Sandra carefully covering the area where the shooting took place. She couldn't find any sign of him, but she placed a call to Mac Farmer and by noon, Farmer, Strong and Brent Wilkes were on the property.

"You okay?" Mac asked.

"I'm good. I know I hit him with that first shot, he rolled. I couldn't have been more than thirty yards away when I fired."

"Not sure I could hit a barn at thirty yards in the dark," Strong responded.

"Found a couple of casings in the woods up there, Sandra, .45's?" Brent Wilkes walked out of the woods from where Sandra had fired with three bullet casings in his hand.

"They're mine."

"I measure about eighty feet to here," Wilkes told the group.

"I can't believe it, there's nothing here, if not blood, then some cloth or something?" Sandra looked at Brent.

"If he was wearing a K-15 vest with a plate, your .45 wouldn't even leave a mark."

"What's a K-15?" Sandra asked.

"They have a new synthetic fiber called Kevlar," Strong responded, "stronger than steel. They weave four or five layers into a vest and your .45 would never get through."

"Would we be looking for a Marine then?"

"No absolutes, but in this area, I'd be leaning that way," Brent offered his opinion.

"I start with NIS tomorrow morning," Strong said, "let's see where that goes."

"I've asked for surveillance on John Holly, I'm waiting on the background check now," Farmer added.

"Sandra, let's go see if we can find his bullet," Brent started walking up the hill. The others followed and once Brent was in the trailer he had Strong and Farmer help him run string from the window to the hole in the back wall of the trailer, it helped him to determine the trajectory of the bullet. He slid the string through the hole and with the other two men helping to keep the line straight, he walked about twenty feet into the woods and found the spot where the bullet entered a pine tree.

"Got it!" He carefully dug it out of the tree and placed it in his gloved hand. Mac, Derrick and Sandra came out the back door of the trailer.

They looked at the bullet in Brent's hand, "Don't touch," he cautioned.

"Damn Sandra, this guy doesn't like you at all," Mac commented.

Sandra looked at the men, "What's wrong?"

Brent looked at Sandra, "This guy wasn't hunting deer, Sandra. See the black tip on the bullet, this is an armor piercing round. It went through your glass window, some plastic, the interior wall, some sheet metal and that tree." Brent pointed at a tree about twelve feet closer to the trailer. There was an exit hole on the back of the tree. "If this was a hunter, he would have used a soft nose round, like a Remington Core-LokT, when it hit the trailer it would have mushroomed up. This thing is almost intact." He smiled, "Maybe I'll get a print off this."

Puzzle Pieces

"We're back to military?" Sandra asked.

"Yes. Time to find out where the Commander was last night," Strong grumbled.

Sandra looked at Strong, "Derrick, you could screw this thing up if you're not careful," she smiled, that infectious smile.

Strong smiled back, *Touché.*

"Sandra, you're going to Raleigh, on Friday?" Mac asked.

"Right."

"Why don't you stop by the office on the way up, around 10am? We can update you then and maybe you can show us how that cube thing works," Mac said with a straight face.

******

Sandra spent the rest of Wednesday and Thursday morning replacing the glass in the window and repairing the holes in her trailer, both the inside and outside walls. Thursday afternoon she picked up her mail at the Post Office in Swansboro. Jenny's package was there. She stopped at a few stores in Swansboro and then headed home. She spent Thursday night wrapping gifts and packing. Friday morning she drove to Jacksonville. She made one stop on the way to the SBI office.

"So what have you fellas got?" Sandra asked as the three of them sat down at the conference room table. Sandra opened the two bags she had brought with her and pulled out three coffees, with creams and sugar packs and a box of Krispy Kreme doughnuts.

"Outstanding!" Mac said loudly, "My favorite."

"Help yourselves guys, now what have you got?"

"We have a bottle of ether missing from the inventory at the base hospital. And we have a Commander that was up to his ass with patients Tuesday night. He's not the shooter, Sandra," Derrick sipped his coffee.

"How about John Holly?"

"Originally, from Fayetteville. Divorced from his wife after seven years, she was cheating on him. Other than that, clean as a whistle, not even a traffic ticket. We have him under surveillance," Mac responded as he started his second doughnut.

"Could these two guys be working together?"

"Highly unlikely. These two seem to be stand up guys, Sandra. We think it would be freakishly rare for both of them to go nuts at the same time, given their backgrounds."

"So, what I hear you guys saying is that after two weeks, we have two dead woman, two dead dogs, two attempts on my life, two cleared suspects and two agents without any leads?"

"You forgot the two doughnuts Mac just ate," Strong pointed at Farmer.

"Did Brent get anything off that bullet?"

"No, wiped clean," Strong continued, "Sandra, you have to understand, we're really in the early stages here. I don't think we've ruled out either of them completely, we're just going to have to—"

"How about that vest, are there any missing from the base? How about the bullet he shot through my trailer, any of that ammo missing?"

"We're working with NIS, Sandra, it will take time."

The three of them talked for awhile, but nothing new developed and Sandra could feel the men's frustration. She pulled a pack of cigarettes out of her purse and lit one. She slid the pack with the lighter over in front of Strong. He took one, lit it and sent them back.

"Thanks."

"Okay, you guys need some time. I could use a break myself. I'll be at Lane's until next weekend. I hope you enjoy the holiday."

"Thought we were going to get some help from you today, Sandra?"

She looked over at Farmer and he tossed the cube across the table. Sandra caught it. She looked at the cube, the colors were all mixed together; she stood up. Her hands flashed quickly as she turned the cube, in about thirty seconds she showed it to Mac. All the colors were aligned.

"Impressive."

Sandra turned the cube again scrambling the colors, then she tossed it back to Mac. "Keep at it, you'll figure it out. Merry Christmas."

Christmas in the Fast Lane

Sandra pulled up in front of Lane's house, it was all decorated with white lights and spotlights, it looked beautiful. She got out of her truck as Jenny opened up the front door.

"Hey, Jenny!"

The two embraced.

"Need some help?" Jenny offered. Before Sandra could respond, Jenny reached into the truck and picked up Jerry. "Hi, Jerry! Remember me, I'm the one with the food." Jerry purred. Jenny grabbed the cat cage in her left hand and closed the door with her hip.

Sandra pulled her purse, a suitcase, a dress bag and a shopping bag with gifts out and they went into the house. The huge center hall was decorated with small white lights and beautiful green wreaths, with pinecones and red ribbons, the grand stairway banister was wrapped with green garland, small white lights and pinecones.

"It's beautiful, Jenny, it's like you'd envision the north pole, if Santa had money. Must be a lot of work."

"Santa has elves that come in and do this. How about a cup of hot chocolate?"

"You're on. Where's Santa?" The two left the bags at the foot of the staircase and walked back to the kitchen.

"Picking up Sara, they should be here soon. Did you get my package?"

"Yes, and it worked out perfectly, thanks."

Jenny put Jerry up on the huge island counter and ladled out some hot chocolate into two large mugs from a pot of hot chocolate on the stove. She added a scoop of Cool Whip and handed a mug to Sandra. The hot chocolate was delicious. Jerry meowed and Sandra dipped her finger into the Cool Whip, Jerry licked the Cool Whip off her finger as Jenny smiled queerly at Sandra.

"What?" Sandra asked.

"Sandra!" Sara shouted as she and her dad opened the front door. Sara ran back the hallway with a big smile on her face, she turned into the kitchen and stopped. She stared awkwardly at Sandra. Lane walked up behind her.

"I've got this, Sara." He walked over to the stool where Sandra was seated, as she stood up. He extended his arms, bent down and licked the Cool Whip moustache off her face. Then he kissed her. "What a nice Christmas present."

"Oh, Daddy!" Sara walked over and hugged Sandra.

Christmas in the Fast Lane

Sandra looked over at a smiling Jenny, "Thanks for the heads up," she said sarcastically.

"You looked too cute. Who wants hot chocolate?"

Sara sat at the counter beside Sandra. Lane stood on the other side of her as Jenny served. Lane shared his plans for Christmas. "Sandra, we don't overdo the holiday, I mean in terms of presents. We spend some time with charities, attend a party or two and then we usually travel. This year, I'd like all of us to go to Banner Elk. I have a friend who has given me the key to a chalet he has in the area, we can go skiing at Sugar Mountain."

"Oh, Daddy!" Sara smiled at her dad. "This is going to be so much fun!" She turned and looked at Sandra. Sandra looked worried. "What's the matter Sandra?"

"I...I don't know how to ski..."

The other three laughed. "Don't worry Sandra," these two are experts. They'll teach you. If you don't like it, you can sit out on the deck with me. The mountains are beautiful this time of year." Jenny told her.

"I don't have any equipment or clothes to..."

"Sandra!" Sara said firmly. Sandra looked over at her. *Shopping*... Sara sang the word.

Lane put his arm around Sandra, "You're going to let me make you happy aren't you? The way you make us happy?"

She looked up into his blue eyes, what she saw was sincerity. She snaked her arm around his waist, her head pressed into his chest, "You bet."

Sara reached over and grasped Sandra's hand. Sandra turned, "I never had a daughter, but if I had, I'd want her to be just like you." Jenny's eyes met Lane's as he sipped his hot chocolate.

"Can I help with dinner, Jenny?" Sandra asked.

Jenny smiled, "Santa makes all of us happy, Miss Jenny is now on vacation. Where are we having dinner tonight, Santa?"

"The club, at 8pm."

******

"Sandra, come on we have to go!" Lane hollered up the grand staircase.

Sandra stepped out of her guest room and walked to the top of the staircase, "Is this alright?" She asked. She wore a full-collared, red fox fur coat that was contoured at the waist and ran to mid-thigh. The pale red and white fur looked like an extension of her hair, the color was so perfectly matched. Sandra's hands were in the coat's slit pockets and the only other thing visible was a pair of brown alligator pumps she wore. Lane stared at her, his mind racing through various scenarios as she descended the staircase.

When she got to the bottom of the staircase he asked, "Are you wearing something underneath that? Because if you're not, you're going right back up those stairs, and I'm going with you."

In full Sandra Love mode, she turned to Lane, batted her eyelashes and said, "Well, of course I am, Mr. Brendel, what kind of girl do you think I am?"

"Somehow, I'm under the impression that if I live to be a hundred, I'll never know the answer to that question. You are stunning."

"Thank you, and you are far too rich to be that good looking."

Jenny and Sara walked out from the end of the hall where they were retrieving their coats from the coat closet.

"Wow! What a pretty coat, Sandra," Sara admired the coat, "can I touch it?"

"Honey, you can wear it if you want."

"No, I couldn't, no not tonight."

"Sandra, you look wonderful tonight," Jenny added. "Now let's go, before I have to eat one of you."

Lane pulled up in front of the club house and stepped out of the Mercedes. "Good evening, John."

"Good evening, Mr. Brendel." Lane walked around the front of the car as John opened the front passenger door and helped Sandra out. "Good evening, Miss Horne, so nice to see you again."

"Thank you, John."

They went into the club room and were escorted to their table. As they walked to the table, heads turned and Sandra returned the gazes with smiles. Sara was greeted by her girlfriend, Lynda who was dining with her parents. They were seated and ordered dinner. Then Sandra turned to Sara, "Sara, I have something very special for you tonight. I was going to wait until tomorrow night, but your dad told me we might do pizza and that new Star Wars movie tomorrow, so I think this would be the appropriate time. I want you to consider this your birthday and Christmas present." Sandra pulled a small, robin's egg blue box with a white silk ribbon out of her coat pocket and placed it on Sara's empty dinner plate.

Jenny smiled. Lane recognized the box immediately, he shifted uncomfortably in his chair.

Sara looked at the small gift and then at her nana and father.

Lane nodded toward the gift.

"Thank you, Sandra," she said softly. She unwrapped the ribbon and as it fell away the printing on the top of the box was revealed, Tiffany and Co. Sara opened the box and removed the jewelry box inside, she opened it.

"Oh..." Sara gasped as her left hand flew up to her mouth. Inside was an 18k rose gold heart-shaped locket and slider on a matching 18k rose gold chain. Sara's eyes were as big as saucers. "It's so beautiful..." she whispered

"What is it, Sara?" Lane asked.

Sara held up the locket and chain, it glistened in the candle light.

"Wow, Sandra, didn't see that coming," Lane whispered.

Jenny nodded her approval.

"You might want to look inside," Sandra suggested.

Sara opened the locket. She looked at it for a few moments as her eyes began to water, then she jumped up from the table and ran to the ladies room.

"That went well," Lane said sarcastically.

"Excuse me." Sandra got up from the table and followed Sara into the ladies room. No one was in there. She turned to leave, then she heard

Sara crying in one of the stalls. Sandra walked over to the sink and picked up a small hand towel from the neat pile in a small wicker basket on the counter. She ran some water on the then she tapped on the stall door. "Is this going to ruin Christmas, if so, I guess I'll have to go home."

The stall door flew open and banged against the stall wall as Sara threw her arms around Sandra. "I'm sorry...I'm sorry...don't go...Sandra please, don't go...I love you..."

Sandra embraced the young girl for a few moments, "You know I think you and I need some bonding time. I've had time with your dad and your nana, but you and I need to get to know each other better. What do you think?"

"Sandra," Sara released her and stepped back, "you are so much like my Mom. I'm sorry about the scene."

Sandra handed her the towel, "Thank God, I thought it was the picture."

Sara laughed nervously and wiped away her tears. Her hands shook.

"You're shaking," Sandra removed her coat and held it out with one hand, "here."

"Oh...I couldn't..." Sara shook her head negatively. She looked at Sandra's outfit, she wore a tan colored, collared silk blouse, a chocolate mini-skirt and a wide, studded, alligator contour belt with a silver buckle. "You're so beautiful," Sara sniveled.

"As your dad likes to say to me, let me make you happy, it will make me happy." Sandra slipped the fox coat onto Sara. "Now, how about I help you with that." She took the locket from Sara's hands and fastened it around her neck. She turned Sara toward the mirror, "You are gorgeous, and I am hungry. Ready?"

Sara beamed as she looked at herself in the mirror, "Yes, thank you." They walked out into the club room, hand in hand. When they returned to the table Sara let go of Sandra's hand, "Daddy, Nana, look." She showed them the locket. When she opened it up there were two pictures inside, cut to fit. The pictures were head shots of Sara and Sandra in the forest, smiling.

Dinner was served. Lane asked Sara to say grace. Sara responded by extending her hands. The four held hands as Sara offered up a slower and more heart-felt prayer than Sandra had heard before. As they ate, Sandra turned to Lane, "Sara and I reached an accord while we were in the ladies room."

"And..." He responded. Jenny's head came up.

"She has agreed to take good care of me when we go skiing and in return, I will be spending more time with her this weekend. It's a chic thing."

The Return of Sandra Love

Sara smiled and turned to her nana, "We're going to do some bonding, Nana, okay?"

"Sara, that sounds like a great idea."

They finished dinner and Sara asked if she could be excused to show her locket to Lynda. After she left, Lane turned to Sandra, "Tiffany's for a fifteen year old?"

"You disapprove?"

"Lane!" Jenny stated sharply.

Lane turned toward Jenny. The older woman leaned forward, "Sandra and I planned this together, so I wouldn't go there if I were you. The gift is inside the locket, do you understand?"

"I just don't want to raise some spoiled rich gir—"

"Lane, all three of us screwed this up." Sandra cut him off. "Thanksgiving we spent getting to know each other, and Lane, you and I had time at the coast. Based on what just happened, it might be time for Sara and I to talk. She said that I was so much like Annie and that she loved me. We're going to have to deal with that together, we were all worrying about our own vulnerability and we forgot about hers."

"Jesus, Sandra, you are like Annie," Jenny gasped, "you even think like she would."

"Okay, but no more expensive gifts, agreed?" Lane asked.

"Lane, I didn't pay a cent for that, you know that. We had a conversation about men and money, you know my background and how I feel about it. You take me shopping and skiing and bring me here to this club, then you worry about a locket with my picture inside. How much have you had to drink?"

Lane backed off, "No. I was affected by that damn outfit you're wearing and didn't have capacity at the time, your honor."

Sandra smiled, "Now there's my Billy Flynn."

Jenny laughed at the rather obscure reference to the character from the Broadway musical, "That's right, you're from Chicago."

"One more thing, then we've beat this horse enough," Sandra said as she reached under her chair. "Jenny, I'm going to have to take your gift back." She placed the gift on the table within Jenny's reach.

Jenny grabbed it, "If this is from Tiffany's, it stays."

"It's not from Tiffany's, you told me what you wanted for Christmas the first time we met."

Jenny's expression reflected her lack of memory, she opened the gift.

"What is it?" Lane asked.

Jenny looked at the toy car, "I'll be damn! You got me my Mercedes!"

"Do I get something?" Lane inquired.

"Your gift comes later," Sandra replied.

******

Saturday morning Lane and Jenny went to deliver presents to the children's unit at WakeMed Hospital. The gifts were contributed by Lane's staff and clients. Sandra and Sara stayed behind, this morning was their time together. They sat in the sunroom with orange juice and hot chocolate.

"Sara, before we start, I only have two rules. First, no lies. All friendships are based on trust, never lie to a friend, okay?"

"Okay."

"And second, this is our private conversation, only you and me, no one else. If that trust is broken, so is our friendship. Understand?"

"Yes."

"Why don't you go first, Sara, what would you like to know about me?"

"Everything."

"Well, we only have a whole day and I'd like to get to know you too."

"Are you and my dad, you know...doing it?"

Sandra stared in disbelief, "That's a hell of a first question," Sandra paused, "today is your fifteenth birthday, have you taken up with boys yet?"

Sara's eyes got wide and she whispered, "I have a boyfriend, Nana and Daddy don't know. I see him over at Lynda's, he lives next door to her."

"Are you doing it with him?"

"Sandra!"

"Remember how you feel right now, Sara, ladies and gentlemen don't talk about their lovers, ever. Never, ever."

"Can I ask you how old you were when you first did it?"

"Sure, fifteen."

"Fifteen! Who was he, was he good looking?"

"I was raped and beaten by two men when I was fifteen. Neither one of them was particularly good looking."

"What happened?"

"I made a mistake and no one was there to help me. They caught the two men and they went to jail, but it was a mistake that changed my life."

"Can I ask you how old you were when you first made love with someone?"

"Sure. I was seventeen, his name was Frank, he was ten years older than me. Most of what I know about sex, I learned from him. I married him when I was eighteen, much too young. I had my son when I was nineteen and we separated that year. Sara, there is one thing I can share with you about sex and men. I want you to remember this before we move on. There is a big difference between making love and sex. Take my word on that, I know what I'm talking about. You're fifteen, you're becoming a woman, you have all these hormones running around inside you and you're curious, that's perfectly normal. These things create desire, a very strong desire. The instinct to promulgate the species is second only to the instinct to survive, that's God's design. But we're not animals, we're at the top of the food chain. We live in a society that has morals and acceptable behaviors. As a woman, in our society, you decide, but if you make the wrong decision many people in our society will shun you. Making love is an art, and should always reflect a deep love and commitment to your partner, sex should be fun and gratifying to you and your partner. The two are often confused, you should wait until you are mature enough to discern the difference."

"Can I ask you something about what you just said?"

"Sure."

"That part about gratifying, what's it like?"

Sandra giggled at the pure innocence of Sara's question.

"Pretty damn good. Tell you what, this conversation should really be between two people who know each other better. Let's get to know each other better, then we can talk about sex, deal?"

"Deal! Daddy said you use to work for the FBI, did you ever shoot anyone?"

Sandra paused, as she reflected on her life and Sara's difficult questions. *This isn't getting any easier, maybe I should have stayed with the sex.*

"Yes, it was self defense and in the line of duty. It is something that is always with me. When I pass, I hope God will forgive me."

"Do you think there really is a God?"

Suddenly, Sandra felt herself facing a fight or flight decision. "Damn, Sara, do you have these questions written down somewhere? I didn't study for this test."

"I thought about them a lot last night when I was in bed, looking at my locket." Sara reached down and rubbed the rose-gold heart between her thumb and forefinger, she kissed it gently. "If Mom was here I'd ask her, I just don't feel comfortable with Nana, and I could never ask Daddy."

"Yes. The answer to your question is yes. I think of him as a friend and I like talking to him directly, it always makes me feel comforted. Every person has to decide for themselves, if occasionally you're faith is weak, don't be fooled, that's the devil's trick. Can I ask you a question?"

"Sure."

"Do you know that I lost my mom from cancer about the same time you lost yours?"

"NO!"

"I loved my mother very much, Sara. I have many friends, but no one will ever be able to take her place. Do you understand what I'm saying?"

Sara was silent for awhile as she thought about what Sandra had just told her. Sandra sipped her hot chocolate and lit a cigarette. As she smoked she watched Sara, the wheels were turning, then Sara's face lit up.

"I'm sorry about your mom, Sandra. You have a very nice way of saying things, without saying them. I think we are going to be BFF's."

"What's a BFF?"

"Best friend forever."

"You bet." Sandra extended her hand. They shook on it.

Sugar Mountain

Sunday, Sandra went to services with Lane and family. They ate breakfast out and left for Banner Elk. They arrived at the A-frame chalet in the afternoon, it was located on the north face of the mountain across the valley from the resort. They did some grocery shopping and cuddled up in front of the field stone fireplace that commanded the center of the great room. The view of Sugar Mountain through the floor to ceiling windows helped put everyone in the Christmas spirit as the ski resort had blown snow over the slopes. They found a cabinet full of board games and played Yahtzee well into the evening before Jenny and Sara retired to their rooms. Lane threw some more wood on the fire and turned off the lights.

"Thanks for the picture, it will go into my office at home. It will remind me of how beautiful you are when we're not together." Sandra had given Lane an 8 1/2"x11" picture of the two of them in the forest. She had framed it in a beautiful gold frame.

"You're welcome. Is there anything else you wanted Santa to bring you?" The two lay on a bear skin rug in front of the fire.

"*Hmmm*...no I think that about covers it," Lane stonewalled.

Sandra sat up, brought her right knee up and rested her chin on it as she stared into the fire, "The man who has everything." The room fell quiet except for the crackling of the fire.

Lane propped himself up on his elbow, reached over and ran his hand through Sandra's hair. "If you are here, there's nothing else I want." He gently turned her head and pulled her over to him. They kissed, and he held the kiss as he lay back down on the rug.

Sandra pulled away and looked down at Lane, her hands on either side of his shoulders, her hair hung around her face. "Do you want me?"

"You know I do."

"And you know we are living in the moment and thinking only about ourselves. There are two other people here, I don't want any of us hurt."

"Nor do I, we'll figure it out."

Sandra looked down at Lane for a few moments, then her eyes softened. She pushed back onto her knees. "What do you want from me, Mr. Brendel?"

Lane's smile ran from ear to ear. "Could you do that enchantress thing?"

"Oh, Mr. Brendel, for you, anything." Sandra cooed as she stood up. Lane propped himself up on his elbow again.

"I'll just have to change what I'm wearing."

Slowly, Sandra pulled her top over her head, dropped it behind her and shook her hair out. As she did her cleavage shimmered in the firelight inside her white, silk, demi-cup bra. She reached down to undo the tack button on her jeans, she struggled with it for a few moments and then, "This thing is stuck..." she grumbled. "Oh, I know..." Sandra turned sideways to Lane, took a deep breath and sucked her well-toned belly in accenting her ribcage and thrusting out her breasts. She *managed* to undo the button. She turned back toward Lane and unzipped her jeans.

"Ouch! Damn zipper," she raised her right forefinger as if it had been cut, then she put it in her mouth and sucked on it, her eyes widened. Lane's smile was now frozen on his face. Sandra pushed her jeans down around her knees revealing her white, French-cut, silk panties. She looked down at the floor, "I need to put these clothes up, now where's my top?" Sandra's voice sounded like she was thinking out loud and unaware that anyone else was present. She turned her back on Lane, "Oh there it is..." Sandra bent over from the waist to pick up her top, and show him her ass.

"That's enough!" Lane jumped up, ready to go. "I know when I'm being had!" He grabbed Sandra and turned her around.

The Return of Sandra Love

"Mr. Brendel, did I do something wrong?"
Sandra was not letting go of the fantasy.

Lane swooped her up in his arms, "Nope! I'll
take it from here!" He laid her down on the rug
and pulled her jeans off. Sandra lay on the black
rug in her bra, panties and white ankle socks.
Lane looked down at her as he took his clothes
off. He lay down gently on top of her, "Merry
Christmas, Sandra."

Sandra closed her eyes, turned her head
exposing her neck, and arched her back slightly,
"Merry Christmas, Mr. Brendel," she whispered.

******

Monday, December 22 was a bright sunny day
in Jacksonville, but a cold front had come in and
the normally mid-fifties highs were replaced with
a brisk wind and an upper-thirties forecast.
Evelyn Martin pulled her coat collar up as she
stepped out of Luigi's, crossed the street and
walked down Court Street toward her business.

I know I'm getting old now, she thought, *not use
to this weather.*

VAROOOM!

The sound of the car accelerating behind her
sounded out of place as the speed limit was
25mph on Court Street's narrow pavement.

THRURMP!

"What the hell..." The noise behind her sounded like a car had hit something in the road, it startled her and she wheeled around to see what was happening.

A car had hit the curb and jumped up on the sidewalk, it was bearing down on her at a high rate of speed!

"Oh nooo..."

WHUMP!

Before Evey could take a step, the car hit her! Her body flew through the air twenty feet and landed with a sickening crunch in an empty lot a half a block from her brothel. She rolled over and over as the car continued down the sidewalk, veered back onto the street and disappeared around the corner. Her twisted body lay still.

******

"Mr. Brendel, great to see you again. Hi, Sara, Miss Jenny." The owner of the ski shop greeted the four as they walked into the store. "How can I help you today?"

"Grant, this is a very dear friend of mine, Sandra Horne. She's joined us for the week and we need to outfit her."

The owner extended his hand, "Nice to meet you, Miss Sandra."

The Return of Sandra Love

Sandra shook his hand, "Nice to meet you too, Grant. Sandra is fine."

He smiled, "So what are we talking about, skis, boots and apparel?"

"She's a first-timer. We'll rent the equipment at the lodge, but we need to outfit her, everything."

"Well, let's get you fitted up, Sandra." The three of them moved toward the clothing racks as Sara and Jenny browsed. Sandra took her green parka off and Grant took her measurements before they started trying on outfits. Sandra took a pair of ski pants, sweater and jacket into the dressing room and returned. She stood in front of a three-way mirror in a white cotton turtle neck, navy blue sweater, red CB Jacket and a pair of bulky, navy blue ski pants.

"I feel like I'm back in elementary school, in Chicago," Sandra commented to Lane. Sara stood behind Grant shaking her head negatively.

"Grant, do you have anything, new?"

"Yes, just in, but very high end."

"Bring it on."

Grant went into the back of the store and returned with a white coat and black bib ski pants. The coat had connected red and black side stripes from the waist to under the arms and matching stripes on the sleeves that ran from shoulder to cuff. He turned the coat around,

214

on the back was a small insignia of a black widow spider.

Sandra's face lit up.

"This is a new company, Spyder. They're located in Boulder, Colorado, and they're outfitting the US Ski Team. They have this new lining called Thinsulate, you won't need the sweater with this. The pants are bibs, but not full bibs, I think you'll like them, Sandra. This is what the best skiers in the world are wearing."

Sara and Jenny walked over as Sandra took the outfit to the dressing room. She returned beaming. She wore the white turtle neck, black bibs that contoured between her breasts and then curved out into two shoulder straps and the jacket that fit like a glove. She spun around as she smiled.

"Freedom! And they're very warm, I'm not wearing my jeans! Oops!" Sandra put her hand over her mouth and giggled.

"You might want to pick up a pair of long underwear, it gets cold on that mountain. We have some very nice Damarts for women," Grant suggested, "the coat comes with a removable hood, it's in the back with the box."

Sara nodded affirmatively as Sandra's enthusiasm grew.

They picked out the thermal underwear, goggles and ski gloves, then Sara, Jenny and Sandra picked out headwear. Sara bought some ear warmers that fit over her thick curly hair, Jenny picked a traditional ski hat with big snowflakes, but Sandra couldn't resist a white bomber hat with faux fur ear flaps and bill. Grant bagged the clothes she wore into the store and they all left ready for the slopes.

"Thank you, Lane, I hope I don't break my leg on my first try after you spent all that money."

"Sandra, if you never even go up the slope, it was still worth the money. You look great. Now, who's ready for lunch?"

They had lunch at the lodge and then after buying their passes, Sandra was fitted with boots, skis and poles. Sara, Sandra and Lane walked over to the beginner's hill, as Jenny waved at them from the deck that overlooked the base of the mountain. Sandra felt awkward walking in the ski boots. They stepped into their skies and Sandra was confronted with her first challenge. A rope tow led to the top of the beginners slope.

"Sandra, I'm going to go first, then you, then Daddy. What's the only thing you have to remember?"

"Don't cross the tips of my skis!"

"Perfect!" Now let's practice moving sideways on your skis. It's not crowded so you have plenty of time to move to the rope before you grab it."

They practiced for a few minutes and then it was time to go. Sara edged herself over to the tow rope and before she grabbed it, she turned to Sandra, "I'll wait for you at the top, when you get there, let go and snow plow like I showed you!" She put her poles under her left arm and grabbed the moving rope, it whisked her away up the slope.

Sandra moved tentatively over to the rope. Lane was behind her. "When you grab the rope it will pull you forward, bend your knees and keep your weight back," he advised as he bent his knees and showed her the correct position.

Sandra tucked her poles and looked at the rope. It looked like it was moving a million miles an hour. *Don't cross you tips,* she thought and grabbed the rope. The rope jerked her forward and she almost fell flat on her face, but she bent her knees and the rope started to pull her up the hill. She looked down, her skis were parallel in two shallow ruts made by previous skiers, with little chance of crossing, she took a deep breath, "I did it!"

When she got to the top she could see Sara in a flat area off to the right at the top of the hill, a slight slope led down to where she waited. A young man stood to her right at the rope tow control. As the terrain flattened the rope curved off to the right on the return run down the hill. Sandra released the rope and started to slide down the slope, her skis parallel. She started to pick up speed.

"Snow plow, Sandra! Snow plow!"

Sandra approached Sara, "How do I stop?" She shouted, all her new found confidence, gone.

"Spread your legs wider and snow plow, Sandra!"

Sandra spread her legs wider apart and turned her tips in, she started to slow, but she was headed straight for Sara and wasn't going to stop before she ran into her. Sara planted her poles on either side of her and jumped around so that her skis pointed straight up the hill, she started to slide backwards down the hill. Sara shifted her tips out and she slowed as she performed a reverse snow plow. Sara held out her hands and Sandra drifted gently into her arms, then Sara turned her so they were perpendicular to the hill.

"Relax, girlfriend, remember our deal, I gotcha," Sara smiled.

"You didn't tell me you were that good!" Sandra's heart was beating like a rabbit's as Lane pulled up beside them.

"You okay?"

"I'm in good hands." Sandra looked down the hill. "This is pretty high."

"I'll have you at the top by tomorrow," Sara shouted as she pointed at some skiers in chair lifts on their way to the top of the mountain. Sara and Sandra skied down the hill, Sara in reverse snow plow as she held Sandra's hands and showed her how to turn by shifting her weight to her outside leg and using her poles to brace. She explained how opening and closing the wedge her skis made while snow plowing would make her go slower or faster. When they got to the bottom they poled over to the rope tow, where Lane waited.

"I haven't had this much fun since never." Sandra said.

Lane looked at her rosy red cheeks. "You look happy."

"I am."

They did two more runs traversing the slope with Sara skiing backwards in front of Sandra, then Sandra wanted to try it on her own. Sara told her to follow her down the mountain and Sandra agreed. She followed Sara's extra slow snow plow down the slope and made it on her own. As she poled over to the rope tow, she waved at Jenny as she watched from the deck.

"Okay, you're ready." Sara told her as they stood at the top of the hill for another run. "Three things, if you lose control, sit down."

"Got it."

"If you fall, remember your skis must be across the slope before you try to stand up."

"Okay."

"And third, you go first."

Sandra looked down the hill, she was excited, but a bit nervous. She bent her legs and pushed off. Slowly, she crossed the slope, her turns acute so her speed was slow, but after a couple of crosses she pointed her skies on a less acute angle and her speed increased. She shifted her weight and turned again and her speed slowed. *I'm getting the hang of this,* she thought. She made it down the hill and stopped. She looked up the hill and saw Lane and Sara paralleling the hill side by side. It was beautiful to watch. As she watched she thought, *Be strong, Sandra, this fantasy can't last forever.*

The two came to the bottom of the hill quickly and directly at Sandra. About ten yards away they twisted toward each other and *hokey stopped* into Sandra, spraying her with snow.

"That wasn't very nice," Sandra said as she cleaned the snow off her goggles and cheeks.

"Oh Sandra, it's a hockey stop. If you take someone skiing for the first time and they don't fall once, it's a salute to their rare accomplishment. Welcome to the club." Sara extended her hand.

Sandra shook her hand and smiled. "It's only because I had the best teacher ever!"

"Wait a minute, don't I get credit here?" Lane asked.

"You'll get what's coming to you later." Sandra put the end of her pole on her releases, pushed down and stepped out of her skis. Then they joined Jenny in the lodge.

******

The next two days found the three of them skiing while Jenny played cards in the lodge. Tuesday afternoon they took Sandra to the top of the mountain on the chair lift. The scenery was beautiful and after a few runs she was on her own. She fell twice and learned from each fall, but her joy was the serenity of the mountains and the great outdoors. On Wednesday, Christmas Eve, they were having a late lunch in the lodge when Lane was paged over the loud speaker. He left the table to answer the page.

"Sandra! Sandra Love?"

Sandra looked up. A very good looking young man in his late twenties stood a few feet away, next to him was a beautiful young woman with long blonde hair, she looked Scandinavian.

"Oh my God!" Sandra's hands flew up to her face. "Jake, my Jake?"

"No, Sandra, it's me Joey." He pulled off his ski hat, his thick black hair tumbled down to his shoulders. "Jake's little brother, Joey. I thought it was you when you took off your hat and I'd know those green eyes anywhere."

"Joey, Oh my God, I haven't seen you in ten years. How are you doing?"

"I'm good. It was the New Years Eve party at The Court, I was nineteen. This is my fiancé, Ingrid."

"Nice to meet you, Ingrid. These are my friends, Jenny and Sara."

Joey and Sandra exchanged pleasantries and then she asked him if they could talk privately. They sat down at a table on the other end of the deck.

"Joey, how is Jake?"

"He's fine. He works for a movie company in Wilmington, he handles transportation for the company. He got married four years ago, her name is Cindy, and she has green eyes. After the trial, he told me about the two of you, he loved you a lot Sandra. I think you broke his heart."

"Joey, I loved your brother very much, he saved my life, him and Jerry Crosby Miller. Is Jerry still around?"

"No, there was a shoot out a few years ago between him and four drug dealers, Jerry killed all of them, but they also got him."

"How about Billy Arrowood? What's it like in Newport these days?"

"Billy's good. I see him walking from time to time. I think there will always be some moonshine boys doing business, but the drugs and prostitution is on the decline. We have some honest people in charge now and that makes a big difference. It all started with you, Sandra, you're like an urban legend, only rural."

Sandra smiled. "That's nice."

"Sandra, you don't ever want to come back though, I think the Yocum's have a reward for your head."

"That's one of the reasons I wanted to talk to you. I'm in the witness protection program, I don't work for the FBI anymore. You know how important it is that no one ever hears about our chance encounter."

"I'll explain it to Ingrid on the way home tonight, but I can't not tell Jake."

Sandra stood up, so did Joey. "You tell him I send him my love, all my love." She hugged Joey tightly.

Joey leaned down and whispered in Sandra's ear, "Yea, well I use to think about you a lot when I was younger." He pulled back and smiled, his face so similar to Jake's.

"You Dawson boys sure aren't hard to look at."

"Sandra."

Sandra turned as Lane approached.

"Take care, Sandra."

"You too, Joey." Joey left.

"That was Jake's brother. My Jake, from Newport."

"Everything going to be alright?" Lane asked as he turned and watched Joey and Ingrid as they headed toward the exit.

"It's cool. Business call, on Christmas Eve?"

"Sandra, please sit down, we need to talk for a minute."

"What's wrong?" She asked as they both sat at the table.

"Evelyn Martin was the victim of a hit and run on Monday. That was Mac Farmer on the phone. She's in Jacksonville hospital, she's in a coma and fighting for her life."

"That bastard!" Sandra's face showed her anger as she balled her hands into fists on the table.

"They found out about it Monday night on the news. He's been trying to get in touch with you since yesterday. He said if she comes out of the coma, you should be there."

"I understand."

"He gave me his home phone in case you wanted to talk. I told him we were headed back on Friday. This is your call, Sandra, if you want to go back tonight, we will."

Sandra extended her hands across the table and gripped Lane's. "That is so sweet of you, but until she comes out of the coma, there's really nothing I can do. I'd rather be with you on Christmas, than be alone."

Lane smiled, "It's getting dark, let's go eat."

As the four of them walked to the Jeep, Sara asked Sandra, "Why did he call you Sandra Love, Sandra?"

Lane and Jenny looked at Sandra.

"Because that's my middle name."

The Return of Sandra Love

Traps, Pitfalls and Swindles

The snow began to fall around 8pm. The outdoor flood lights at the chalet provided a beautiful view of the snow falling in the Blue Ridge Mountains of North Carolina on Christmas Eve. Sandra stood in front of the chalet's windows with a cup of hot chocolate and a mind full of memories. Her year in the mountains, her Christmas in the forest, her family so scattered and gone. Lane had put an album of Christmas carols on the stereo, Silent Night added to the Christmas card panorama in front of her.

"Penny for your thoughts," Lane stepped up beside her and slipped his arm around Sandra's shoulders, she put her arm around his waist.

"You don't have enough money," she replied as she put her cup down on an end table and turned toward him, "I could use a hug."

She embraced Lane as he put his arms around her. She slipped her left hand up on to the back of his neck bent his head gently and planted a lip lock on him with every ounce of emotion that raced through her body. She held the kiss forever.

"Save some water for the camels, Sandra!" Jenny exclaimed. She and Sara were working on a snow scene puzzle at the kitchen table.

"They look like the cover on those romance novels you read, Nana," Sara whispered as she watched her father and Sandra together in front of the picturesque front windows.

"Yes..." Jenny said softly as she turned her head back to the puzzle.

******

Christmas morning, Lane woke up to an empty bed. He showered, dressed and came out into the kitchen.

"Juice in the fridge, coffee's in the pot," Jenny told him. "Grab some doughnuts, we're going on a hike this morning when Sandra's through with the coleslaw."

Sandra was shredding cabbage while Sara peeled potatoes. The small turkey they bought was stuffed with bread stuffing, sitting on the counter next to the oven. Jenny was cleaning up the kitchen.

"How much snow did we get?"

"Four or five inches, it's tapering off now," Sandra replied as Lane walked to the windows.

They finished the prep work for dinner and went for a hike in the woods, Sandra led. A few hundred yards up the mountain Lane hollered, "Hold up, Sandra!"

Sandra stopped. The other three caught up.

"I think your pace may be a bit fast for Jenny," Lane told her.

"I'm sorry, Jenny," Sandra looked at Jenny, she was bent over and breathing hard."

"If I die out here, it will just ruin Christmas," Jenny huffed.

"Take a break for a few minutes, I'll see if I can find a bench where the walking will be easier."

"Try and find one I can sit down on," Jenny stood up straight and looked at Sandra smiling at her double entendre.

"Will do." Sandra started up the hill picking her way through the trees and blow downs. Another fifty yards up she stepped up onto a wide bench with deer tracks and droppings. She walked across the bench and looked back, she couldn't see the others. She walked farther out along the bench.

"Lane, come on up!"

"That's Sandra, sounds like she found some easy walking, let's just go slow. We're not in any rush." Lane started up the mountain, Jenny and Sara followed. They got to the bench and started to follow Sandra's fresh prints in the snow. They talked as they walked. The snow was wet and every twig on every branch of every tree was adorned in Christmas white. After they had walked a bit, Lane looked down at the snow, the footprints stopped.

"Sandra!" Lane hollered.

"Where did she go, Daddy?" Sara's face looked tense.

"Lane?" Jenny's voice was unsure.

Lane smiled, "Ladies, we've been had. Turn around." The three of them turned and ten feet behind them stood Sandra.

"Hi."

"Sandra!" Sara raced back to her. "How did you do that?"

Sandra laughed, "Ask your daddy."

"She back tracked on us Sara," Lane said as he and Jenny walked back to where the other two stood. "First you find somewhere you can step off the path without your tracks being noticed, like behind that tree." Lane pointed at the large tree Sandra had hid behind. "Then you walk down the path past that point and step backwards into your own footprints. A good tracker will pick up the trail quickly, but that's not why you do it."

"Why do people do it then?" Sara asked.

"It gives them the element of surprise. In war, we would all be dead right now."

"Don't shoot the old woman!" Jenny said, "You can just hike me out this mountain a little more and leave me for dead."

"Well, here's the good news, Jenny, it's all flat walking from here to the point, then it's an easy walk back and all downhill to the house." Sandra told her.

"Okay, sign me up."

After walking in the forest the four returned to the cabin and ate their Christmas dinner. After dinner Lane and Sandra put their coats on and stepped out on the front deck. Sandra lit a cigarette as Lane lit his Cuban cigar.

"I have an idea on how to catch this bastard," Sandra started, "we need to isolate him, set a trap and spring it. Just can't do that in Jacksonville."

"Where?" Lane asked.

"In my neck of the woods," Sandra smirked.

Lane looked at his lady as he thought, *I wonder what the hell is going on in her mind.*

******

On the 26th they skied the morning session at Sugar Mountain, ate lunch and drove back to Raleigh. Sandra called Mac on the way home; Evelyn was still in a coma. She told him she wanted to talk to the two of them first thing Monday morning. As they drove, Sandra turned to Lane, "I'm going back Sunday night."

"I have to go into the office Monday, but I'd like us to talk when we get home."

"Do you have to go, Sandra?" Sara asked from the back seat.

"Yes, Sara, I have some important business back home I need to take care of Monday."

"We've enjoyed your company this week, Sandra, hope you can make it back up soon," Jenny added. She rubbed her hand gently on Sara's leg.

Saturday morning Lane and Sandra came down to the kitchen around 8am.

"I thought I smelled breakfast, outstanding!" Lane looked down at the pan of scrambled eggs with ham and cheese, the stack of blueberry pancakes Jenny was making and the sausage.

"Sandra, can you get Sara up?" Jenny asked.

"Sure." Sandra headed toward the hall.

"About five minutes, Sandra," Jenny added.

Sandra made her way up to Sara's room and knocked on the door. No answer. She opened the door quietly. Sara lay on her right side across her queen-size white, princess bed. Her right leg was under the sheet and comforter, but her long left leg was exposed on top of them. The tall willowy young woman rested

She wore a pair of panties and an NC State football shirt. She was spooning with her pillow. Sandra walked quietly around the bed to where she could see Sara's face. Sara looked like a princess. Her thick curly hair hung around her perfect little face in cascades. Sandra looked at her, *No wrinkles and no worries*, she thought. She sat gently on the side of the bed and stroked Sara's hair. Sara's big brown doe eyes opened and she looked at Sandra, then they closed again. Sandra picked up one of the throw pillows on the floor.

WHOMP! She smacked the pillow down on Sara's head.

"Sandra!" Sara rolled over away from her antagonist.

WHOMP! WHOMP! WHOMP!

Sara jumped out of the other side of the bed and armed herself with two throw pillows that were on the floor. "You asked for this!" She swung her arms around like windmills. "I must warn you, I took Karate last semester."

"And I must warn you, I took it for four years!"

"Sara let go of her pillows and they flew at Sandra's face. Sandra easily parried them away.
"Not through the Iron Duke!" Sandra ran at Sara and threw the pillows at her face. As Sara blocked them, Sandra stooped under her taller opponent stuck her hand between Sara's legs

and grabbing her right arm hoisted Sara up onto her shoulders in a fireman's carry.

"And now little girl, it's off to *The Kingdom of the Kitchen* where I will sell you to pirates for gold! *BWAHAHA...*"

"No...no...not the dreaded ECU pirates!" Sara screamed and laughed as Sandra carried her out of the bedroom and down the hall to the top of the staircase. "Help...Daddy...help... me...*EEEEEEK,*" Sara screamed at the top of the staircase and then laughed and giggled as Sandra descended the stairs. Lane and Jenny heard the commotion and came running out.

Sandra reached the bottom of the staircase, turned toward the two and then spoke in a deep male voice, "I have the princess master, I will take her back to The Kingdom of the Kitchen and we can sell her to the pirates."

Lane picked up the cue and took a regal pose, "Excellent work, Igor, but we don't do business with those pirates, summon the gypsies! *BWAHAHA...*"

Sandra put Sara down in the kitchen and the four sat down for breakfast.

"Sandra, you are quick and strong. I wish I could wake up like that every morning." Sara smiled and then started pouring syrup on her pancakes.

The other three looked at each other.

******

Sunday morning Sandra said her farewells to Jenny and Sara as they left for church. Lane had arranged for some time with Sandra. They sat in the family room, Lane in a big leather chair and Sandra on the leather sofa.

"Did you have fun this week?"

"Lane, how could I possibly say no? You made me very happy."

"I might as well get this out of the way now, I'm in love with you."

"Oh, Lane—"

"Let me finish."

Sandra was silent.

"Deeply. I never thought I could ever feel this way again, but I do. We've only known each other a few weeks and I'm a pretty pragmatic guy. I need to know two things from you and I want to share two with you, one of which I just did. The other is that both Jenny and Sara feel the same way I do. Sara says that it's like one of the romance novels that Jenny reads, only real. Jenny said that you are as close to her having a daughter as she will ever feel. This is strong stuff, Sandra, what I need to know from you is, how do you feel about me and do we have a chance?"

The room was quiet for a moment as Sandra reflected. "Before I answer, tell me why you love me, Lane."

He started to get up, "Excellent idea, I'll make a list. Let me get my legal pad out of my office."

"I'm serious, Lane, why?"

Lane sat back down. "Well, let's get the obvious out of the way. You are a beautiful woman and you are great in bed. Now, let's talk about the other less important things." He smiled, but Sandra's face was stern. Lane composed himself and he leaned forward looking directly into her eyes, "You're smart, you have a generousness of spirit, you have a good sense of humor, you make me laugh, you have patience and strength, hang on now, there are others."

"I'll wait."

Lane continued, "You are responsible, you keep confidences, you are refined, you have eclectic tastes, you're not dramatic and you're honest to a fault, but above all of these things, one stands alone, you are trustworthy, and you have won my trust."

"You are very flattering, but I was hoping you'd include—"

"Hold on, I know what you were waiting to hear. I see it in your eyes as we sit here."

"I'm listening."

"And you're not Annie. You are Sandra, you are yourself, and I love you for who you are."

"Oh my God..." Sandra couldn't believe her ears.
"You look astonished. Did you forget I live with two women, I studied for this test."

"You got an A."

"Your turn," Lane waited.

Sandra read his face. "Do I love you? *Hmmm...* well, let's talk about the three prerequisites. You're rich, handsome and know your way around a woman, check! Now we can talk about the less important things."

Lane smiled.

Sandra feigned puzzlement, "I guess that's about it." She watched as Lane's smile ran away from his face.

"Not even a short list?"

"Okay, give me a minute, I'm sure something else will come to me," she teased him.

"Take your time, no pressure."

Sandra stood up and walked over to Lane's chair, she knelt down in front of him, she placed her hands on his thighs. "You are a charming, considerate, brilliant man. You make me laugh,

237

but you also make me think. I've carried my baggage for years, you helped me discard it. You're a spiritual man, but you're not sanctimonious, that is important to me. You live in a very conservative area, yet you analyze issues and people on their individual worth, you're values are the same as mine. You have what I call, personal courage, reflected by the nature of your law practice. And you have a family that has accepted me and shown me love and loyalty in a very short period...for who I am." Sandra stopped for a moment, "Did I mention the sex was good?"

"No."

"It is my love, and we can make this work."

******

Monday morning at 9am Sandra met with Farmer and Strong.

"Good news," Mac began, "Evelyn Martin is conscious."

"What's her condition?"

"Her left hip and leg are broken, she had a grade three concussion, internal bleeding that was repaired with surgery and multiple cuts and bruises."

"Prognosis?" Sandra asked.

"Good with rehabilitation. Her gait may change though, considering her age."

"Security?"

"Jacksonville police, I think some of them are closer to Evelyn Martin than others."

"How about our two friends?"

"At the base, Schneider was working on the schedule he told you. No missing vests or ammo, just the one missing bottle of ether." Strong told her.

"We've had a tail on Holly for a week, nothing. He lives alone in a cabin off Rte 24 in Newport."

"Which side of 24, sound side or forest?"

"Forest."

Sandra smiled.

"I know what you're thinking Sandra, but I just have a gut feeling it ain't him." Mac commented.

"Anything off Evelyn's field cameras?"

"Yes, a rather nasty recording of her body hitting the ground and a few blurry frames of the side of the car, ID impossible, but this we know from the frames we have, it's a black car and it's a big car. John Holly drives a 1969 black Ford LTD."

"Bingo!" Sandra slapped her hand down on the table.

"That's the good news, here's the bad. Brent checked his car out, it has dings and scratches all over it, it's eleven years old you'd expect that, but no blood or other evidence tying the vehicle to the hit and run."

"So maybe he used another car?"

"Well, we'd have to find it first. We're checking car rental companies in the area, nothing yet. We're hoping to find one with tire tread that matches the casts Brent made of the one's you found in the forest, because Holly's tires don't match."

The excitement in Sandra's face waned. "Listen guys, I have a plan."

"We're all ears, Sandra," Mac leaned forward in his chair."

"I think it is much more likely that this guy lives in my area, not in Jacksonville. For whatever reason, he's got this thing going on in his mind about working girls. We don't know when or where he'll strike next, but so far he's taken two of Evey's girls, made a couple of runs at me and now he's taken out the boss. Court Street has a lot more business than just Evey's. Is it fair to assume that this thing he's got in his mind is directly connected to Evey's business and no one else's?"

Strong perked up, "Yes, I'll buy that."

"Keep going, Sandra," she had Mac's attention.

"I need to talk to Evelyn, but maybe we could move her business out of Jacksonville and up the coast to my area. We find somewhere that's somewhat isolated and then we get the word out. It's small town south, it will get out fast. We have to figure out a way where we control the girl's security, then we wait. He will come, he can't stop."

Mac looked at Strong, "It's based on a lot of conjecture, but it's better than anything we have now," Strong responded.

"You'll have to get cooperation from Evelyn Martin and money to make this happen," Mac added. "She's in the hospital and then rehab for the next few months, whose going to run the business?"

Sandra leaned back in her chair and lit a cigarette, she waited.

Mac's face grew stern, "Sandra, do you know how dangerous this would be?"

"That bastard killed my boys, he has no idea how dangerous I can be. Time to decide, gentlemen. Believe me when I tell you I have a better offer on the table in Raleigh. It's this or I'm gone baby gone."

The Return of Sandra Love

Strong stood up, "Go see Evelyn, we'll call the hospital to notify security, she's in Room 308. Find out if she's on board and if there's anything she remembers about the hit and run, let us know. We'll work our end."

"I'll need indemnity for myself and extended to anyone I identify as assisting in the investigation and capture."

Strong smiled, "You really think we'd do that if you were instrumental in catching this guy? The press would eat us alive."

"I heard recently that there's still a contract out on me in Tennessee, I want no mention of me in the press."

"You got it. By the way, we have something for you." He looked at Mac.

Mac reached in his coat pocket and tossed the Rubik's Cube to Sandra. She looked at it. All the colors were aligned.

She smiled and put it on the table, "I'll call you."

******

"Evey, it's Sandra." Sandra stood beside her friend's bed. Evelyn's head was wrapped, her left eye was purple and yellow, she had a large cut across the bridge of her nose, there was a cast on her elevated left leg, a drain tube ran out of her sheets and into a collection bag, she had an IV in her arm and she was wired to a vital signs monitoring system.

Evelyn opened her eyes, she reached out with her left hand, Sandra grasped it and kissed it.

"S-Sandra," she smiled faintly.

"I'm here for you, hon."

"Am...I-I going...to live?" Sandra had to bend over to hear her faint voice.

"I haven't seen your doctor yet. I'm not sure he'll talk to me, without your approval."

"C-call the nurse..."

Sandra buzzed for the nurse. When the nurse came into the room, Evelyn told her that she had no family and wanted Sandra to be treated as her next of kin. The nurse told her that she'd check on how that was done. After the nurse left, Sandra and Evelyn talked.

"That bastard, he fucked me up good, Sandra."

"Evey, is there anything you can remember?"

"Black car and pain. I'm pretty drugged up. What's going on at my house?"

"I haven't been by, who would I talk to?"

Evelyn groaned in pain, "I don't have a succession plan," another faint smile lasted for a fleeting moment, "I-I don't know what will happen to my girls..." Evelyn's eyes moistened.

"Can I help?"

Evelyn squeezed her hand, "I can't ask you..."

"You're not asking, Evey, I am."

"I always liked you, Sandra." Evelyn took a long slow breath. "You got guts. Hand me the phone."

After Evelyn made her call, Sandra placed a call to Lane. They arranged to have a power of attorney document drawn and faxed to the hospital. The document granted permission for health care providers to share Evelyn's health information with Sandra and to require Sandra's approval on all decisions should Evelyn become incapacitated. The document also provided for Sandra's control over Evelyn's business and financial affairs for the next three months. The nurse returned and confirmed the POA was needed. Sandra asked for a fax number and within an hour the document arrived. Evelyn signed the papers. She looked at Sandra, "Take care of them for me, hon."

"I will, Evey, I have a plan."

Interview with the Devil

"They're here, Ma'am." The Jacksonville police officer guarding Evelyn's room announced.

"Thank you, officer, you can let them in." Sandra said quietly. She sat on the far side of Evelyn's bed, she had been reading to her, but she looked down at her friend and Evelyn's eyes were closed.

The two men who walked into the room were intimidating. She put her finger up to her lips, stood up and walked over to the men. "I'm Sandra," she whispered and held out her hand.

"I'm Paul," the black man standing next to her responded. He was about 5'11", but his body was absolute carved granite. He wore a black leather jacket, a black tee-shirt and jeans; he shook Sandra's hand.

"Brian, ma'am, but they call me Cowboy," the white man standing next to him was five inches taller and fifty pounds heavier. He wore a jean jacket, plaid cotton shirt, jeans with a large round belt buckle and a cowboy hat. He looked western.

Big and bad, Sandra thought as she shook hands with Brian, "Nice to meet you. Sandra will do, Cowboy, okay?"

"Yes, ma'am," he caught himself, "sorry, Sandra."

"You two, get over here." They turned toward the bed as Evelyn waved them over with her right arm.

"Hey, Momma Rabbit, how are you doing?" Paul asked softly, as he held her hand.

"Never felt worse in my life, hon. Where's my Cowboy?"

"Here, Momma Rabbit," the big man responded to his nickname.

"You boys pull those chairs over here and sit...*KUHHF...KUHHF...*" Evelyn coughed up some phlegm and Sandra handed her a tissue. The two men sat down. The room was silent for a few moments. Then Evelyn spoke. "We're going to be making a move, sort of like in the Godfather movie. Until I am better, Sandra is in charge of the business, understand?"

"Yes, Momma," Paul responded. Cowboy nodded.

"Sandra and I go back fifteen years, she knows the business well. She's a friend of ours. I want each one of you to give me your word that you will give her your absolute loyalty, no questions asked."

"Yes, Momma," Paul affirmed.

"Cowboy?"

"Always, Momma."

"If there are any problems with the girls, you take it to Sandra." The men nodded. "I'm tired. Sandra will explain the rest."

"Get some rest, Evey, I'll see you soon." Sandra bent over to kiss her friend.

"Sandra, give me your hand." Evelyn took her hand and kissed it as the two men watched the transfer of power, Italian style.

The three rode down in the elevator together, alone. "How many girls do we have now?" Sandra asked.

"Twelve," Paul answered. "Usually, six girls a shift."

"I have some work to do today and tomorrow, but I want to meet with all of them tomorrow at 6pm, no exceptions. Can you do that for me, please?"

"Yes, we'll arrange it."

"Any plans for Wednesday night?"

"New Years Eve, nothing special, both of us are on," Paul replied.

"We're going to have a party, work optional." The elevator doors opened. "What's your favorite restaurant around here?"

247

"We eat at the diner on Rte 17," Cowboy said.

"Come on then, I'll explain what's happening, lunch is on me."

******

"What can you tell us, Sandra?" Paul asked as he started on his steak and salad lunch.

"We're going after this guy. My ex-husband was a Marine, you guys understand Honor, Courage and Commitment?"

"We do," Paul responded, "Sandra, Cowboy and I were in the Corps for twelve years. We got out to go into business together. We had some financing issues, Evelyn bailed us out four years ago. She paid off our debts and made things right for us or we'd be dead now. We owe her our lives."

"And we owe this son of a bitch some pain," Cowboy said, as he clenched his big hand into a fist.

"Let me tell you what I need from you the most, it's secrecy." Sandra went on to explain her plan. She told them that she would be at the brothel every day until they made their move. The men pledged their silence. It was clear, they wanted to nail the killer too.

After lunch she dropped the men off at the hospital parking lot, Sandra stopped at Evelyn's bank to introduce herself. She gave them a copy

of the POA and they had her sign a signature
card for the checking account. She stopped
back at the SBI office and filled the two agents in
on what had happened at the hospital. She told
them about an empty building on Rte 24 in
Bogue that was for rent, it had been a salon, she
thought it would be the perfect spot. There was
a trailer on the property behind the building
where the agents could set up monitoring
equipment. Sandra told them she'd contact the
owner, but would need their help with approval
from local officials, business license and any
code issues. The agents told her they would
handle it, cloaked as an undercover sting
operation for drug dealers. Sandra would run the
business, the agents would monitor it from the
trailer. The next night she met with the girls in
the parlor of Evelyn's house.

"Good evening ladies, my name is Sandra Love,
I'm fine with Sandra. Evelyn and I go back a
long, long time. She has asked me to step in
and run the house for her while she recovers. I
need to know right now, if anyone in this room
has a problem with that."

A Hispanic girl named Maria spoke up quickly,
"If Momma Rabbit wants you to run the show,
that's good enough for us. Just tell us about
yourself and what you're going to do to protect
us from this freak, and is the split still the
same?" The other girls started talking, most of
them affirming the questions.

"Settle down ladies. I run a tight house, would you be acting out if Momma Rabbit was standing here?"

The room went silent amidst some soft spoken no's.

"I started in the business when I was twenty-one. My child was seriously ill, my husband had left us alone and I needed the money to care for my son." Sandra's face was stern. "Any of you ladies know what the fuck I'm talking about?" Sandra shouted as she raised her right fist in unity. The room exploded as the women shouted out their acknowledgement for the familiar scenario. Sandra walked around the room with her right fist in the air as she slapped hands with her left. The women whistled, applauded and nodded their heads in acceptance.

Paul and Cowboy stood in the archway that led to the hall and front door. Paul leaned his head toward his friend and whispered, "That was quick."

After it quieted down, "I worked for the mob for four years, got out of the life, and put myself through college. I moved here, married a Marine and I guess some of you ladies know how that goes, we split last year." Some women laughed others jeered. "Now, I'm here to help my friend and you girls. You have to work to support yourselves, I understand. And you don't want to die." More murmuring. "If you listen to me and follow the rules, you'll make more money, with no risk of injury from this freak. If not, there's the door. How's that sound?"

"What's the plan, Sandra?" Maria followed.

"How many of you have seen the Godfather movie?"

All of them affirmed their viewing.

"We'll be moving *the family* just like Michael Corleone did. We're not going to Las Vegas, we're going up the coast to a house and an area that will be more secure. Paul and Cowboy will handle the logistics if you have transportation problems."

"How do we make more money in a new area?" Another girl asked.

"If you have regulars here, tell them where we're going, they'll follow, you girls know that. It's less than twenty miles away and may be even closer for some of the men who live up there. We'll let them know that the primary reason for this is your safety. What's your split now?"

Several girls answered, "75/25."

"That's going to change." There was some grumbling around the room, then Sandra followed, "While you work for me, I take twenty and you get eighty, but I want you to see that Paul and Cowboy get tipped well, these are the guys that take care of you. Anyone have a problem with that?"

All the girls smiled.

"What's next, Sandra?" Maria asked.

"Tomorrow is New Years Eve, 1981 is going to be a great year ladies. How about we celebrate it tomorrow night with a party, work optional?" The women applauded. Sandra extended her arms. "Group hug!"

The women stood up and they all came over and hugged each other. They spent the next couple of hours planning food and drink for the New Year's party. The party went well and it gave Sandra some time to get to know the women. Thursday, January 1st, they were closed.

On Friday, Sandra contacted the owner of the property on Rte 24. She arranged to meet him and see the property that afternoon, Farmer went with her. They never told him their true interest in the property, but Farmer gave him his card and told him to call if he had any questions. They signed a month to month lease agreement and the owner seemed satisfied with the check Sandra wrote him.

Saturday night Sandra spent the evening at the brothel, she dressed in one of her black cocktail dresses and her green and gold emerald earrings, necklace and ring. She received several proposals from customers, she declined, telling them how flattered she was and giving them a drink on the house.

Sunday was a day of rest. She called Jenny and filled her in on the week's events, spent time listening to Sara whispering about her boyfriend and Lane, tearing himself away from the playoff games. He told her he missed her and worried about her. She thanked him and told him she'd try and see him as soon as she could.

******

Monday, a few minutes before 11am Sandra pulled into the church parking lot. As she was going in, a tall man dressed in jeans and a leather jacket was coming out.

"Jamie, Jamie Howell! How have you been? I was just thinking about calling you." Sandra reached out and shook the man's hand. "I didn't know you were a member here?"

The nice looking man put his finger to his lips, "*Shhh*, Sandra, let's step outside." They stepped onto the sidewalk and he responded, "Good to see you, Sandra, it's been awhile. Actually, I'm...uh...sort of interested in Lisa, if you follow my drift. She's a really a sweet woman."

"Oh, yes, I follow your drift."

"How are you doing? I was sorry to hear about you and Michael splitting up."

"It was a tough year. He's back in Charlotte with his parents. It was difficult for him after he was hurt on deployment."

"Sandra, it happens to a lot of Marines especially the ones with PTSD." As a corpsman, I see a lot of them on base. It's difficult to adjust and there are few programs to help them, they feel alone and discarded. Why were you going to call?"

"I have a friend who's moving her business from Jacksonville to the Crystal Coast, in Bogue, up Rte 24. I was hoping you might put me in touch with those Marines who helped me and Michael when we first moved in. The building is in need of work, she'd be willing to pay them."

"Steve and Ronnie, good guys, but they're on the west coast now."

"Well, if you know of anyone that's looking for some extra money?"

"I'd help you, Sandra, we had a good time getting you guys settled in, but I..." he looked past Sandra toward the entrance to the church office, "to be honest with you, I've been spending time here volunteering for Pastor John and—"

"Hey, I got it," Sandra said as she smiled. "I met Lisa a couple of weeks ago, she seems like a really nice person."

"Thanks, Sandra, that means a lot to me, coming from you. If I hear of anyone who I think can help you, I'll put them in touch. Did you ever get a phone?"

"No, I'll check with some local contractors, she wants to get started next week. Good to see you again, Jamie."

"You too, Sandra."

As the tall man walked over to his car and got in, Sandra's mind started to recall the split with her second husband. She started to feel herself getting depressed. Then she thought, *No more ass kicking, Sandra, if he loved you he wouldn't have left. Be strong!* She went into the office.

"Hi, Sandra," Lisa greeted her, "do you know Jamie?"

"Hi, Lisa, yes I do, good guy."

"I think he likes me."

"I think you may be right, but I don't give advice on matters of the heart, bad track record. Is Pastor John ready for me?"

"Yes I am." Pastor John answered as he came down the hall. "Nice to see you again, Sandra, come on back." As John Holly turned, Sandra pointed at the front door and crossed her fingers, Lisa smiled.

"Please, have a seat."

"Thank you," Sandra sat in front of the desk.

"How can I help you, Sandra?"

"I've had a rather interesting life, Pastor John," Sandra started. She told him about growing up in Chicago, her parents divorcing and her being raped at fifteen. She talked about her son's illness, how she supported herself and getting out of the life to attend college. She skipped over her adventure in Newport, Tennessee, and concluded with meeting her second husband, her mother's death and her recent divorce. "I think I'd like to know your thoughts about good and evil, Pastor John. I've experienced both and been both, I don't know whether I've lived a good life or thrown it away."

"This would be a very short conversation, Sandra, if I responded by telling you, 'Sorry, Sandra, you blew it when you were fifteen.' "

She smiled.

"Tell me about how you see God."

"Well, I think the old white-haired, bearded guy in a long white robe, is most comforting."

John Holly smiled.

"But to be honest, I think that's a bit naive. I think he could be anything he wants to be."

"Let me rephrase, what I was really asking wasn't what he looks like; I was looking for how

you think he thinks. What's his MO, how does he
operate from day to day? What is the meaning
of life? Why are we here?"

"What a great question?" Sandra responded.
She thought for a few moments. "I guess I'm not
a big Old Testament gal, I mean, where did
Cain's wife come from? He married his sister?
I'm not even sure about the New Testament, but
I love the Jesus story."

"So you accept Christ as your savior?"

"I don't know." Sandra felt herself getting tense.
"I think he is someone that we can all emulate,
but do any of us really know? It's a faith thing,
isn't it?"

"Yes, it is. Do you know what it is that makes
your faith weak?"

"Yes."

"Do you want to tell me?"

"I don't like the idea that, if you live a good life,
but don't accept Jesus, you'll burn in hell. What
happens to all the Jews and the Muslims, they
don't get to heaven? I don't like to think about
not seeing my boys again, there are no dogs in
heaven? But I think the big issue for me is the
history of the faith, the crusades, the inquisition,
the witch hunts, so many denominations, it
sounds like a control thing. It's confusing and I
think I'm the kind of person who accepts with

both brain and heart, do you know what I mean, John?"

"Yes I do, and I have some very good news for you. You're not alone."

"Well, that's good to know."

"Sandra, do you believe in God?"

"Absolutely! We're...well...we're...BFF's."

"What is that?"

"Best friends forever."

"Oh, I like that. Can I keep that?"

"Yes you can."

"Thanks. I'd like to share a thought with you, give that brain something to mull over before we meet again."

"Sure."

"All the things you talk about that you say weaken your faith, all human frailties?"

"Yes, go on."

"God's design. If you believe in an almighty God, then it follows that everything here is by his design."

Sandra sat quietly, her head analyzing.

"Remember you told me that you wanted to talk about Good and Evil; both, God's design. Can't have good without evil, there'd be no measurement, right?"

"Right." Sandra whispered.

"So let's talk about his MO, how he sees us, why we're here, his expectations for all his children."

"I'd like to hear about that."

"But before we start, consider this. There may come a time when you or I can't fathom the design, after all, it comes from a brain much greater than ours. At that time, you might want to consider letting you heart, and your faith take the lead."

Sandra's brain was turning, she liked the reasoning that he was presenting, reasoning she had never considered before. She could feel her heart filling with joy as she listened to Pastor John's words.

"So why don't we talk about some of the possibilities of why we're here and what his expectations are?"

Two hours later Sandra walked out of John Holly's office, her only thought was, *It can't be him?*

Over the next few weeks, Sandra arranged for utility services and cleaning and painting inside the building. Mac handled the cameras and trailer, he had them installed after dark and out of site. They covered the entire lot from all angles, including the forest behind the property, and had one face cam at the front door. Inside, the building had a lobby with a counter, an open room to the right that had been used for manicures and pedicures and a half dozen beautician stations in the back separated by walls, but open to the hall. She had doors added to the cubicles and the room on the right which she also had enclosed, it would become the new parlor. Finally, she had a pink street sign made with scrolled black lettering that read:

EVELYN'S
MASSAGE & DAY SPA

Tulip Lane

Time flew by quickly as Sandra was busy
running the brothel, coordinating the move,
visiting Evelyn and meeting with John Holly. She
used Evelyn's private phone to call Jenny and
Lane a couple of times a week. She took Jerry
down to the brothel on Court Street and the girls
fell in love. By Saturday, January 17th, they
were ready to make the move. The furniture
from Court Street, beds, tables, chairs,
television, refrigerator, everything was packed
and ready to go. It was a pleasant day and highs
were expected to be in the upper fifties. The
street sign in front of the new location had a
banner across it with an opening date of Monday
the 19th. The moving van had backed onto the
lot and between the sign and the van, locals
passing by knew the business was opening that
week.

Sandra made sure that there were always a few
girls outside the building, cleaning up the lot or
stringing rope from tree to tree to set up a
parking area. She asked the two black girls, Kim
and Nicky, to dig a hole and set up the mailbox
she had purchased. As the two dug in their tight
jeans, horns started blowing from passing cars.
Sandra watched as the girl's waved and smiled.

The building had a wooden deck behind it
replete with picnic table and chairs. Around 1pm
Sandra had three pizzas delivered. She shared

some with the movers and then she asked the women to join her on the deck. Paul and Cowboy brought a half dozen boxes from the back of Sandra's truck.

"I've put together a schedule based on the preferences each of you gave me." She handed out the schedules to the women. "Any problems?"

After a few adjustments, the women seemed pleased with their working schedules.

"A few weeks ago I asked all of you to give me your measurements and foot sizes. Now I have some gifts for you." Paul and Cowboy started opening boxes. "If you'll line up, Paul and Cowboy will give you yours, then I want you to go into the parlor and put them on. When you're ready come back out and we'll talk."

The women giggled and joked as they lined up to receive their uniforms. They all went into the parlor and changed. Fifteen minutes later they were back out on the deck. Each wore a white tank top with a scooped neckline. The tops had "Evelyn's" scrolled across the front in light pink. They wore Daisy Duke style gym shorts, white athletic socks and white, ankle-high sneakers.

"What do you think?" Sandra asked.

The girls laughed and joked about the new uniforms, most of the comments were about how their shorts showed off their booty. Overall, they liked the way they looked in the uniforms.

"We're in the massage business ladies, here's how it works. You bring your uniforms with you when you come to work and check in at the counter where you will be assigned a booth in the back. You change in the bathroom and wait in the parlor, there's furniture, a TV and a refrigerator in there. Bring some reading material if you don't watch TV. Customers will come in and after they pay at the counter, they will be escorted into the parlor by Paul or Cowboy. The customer enters and picks his masseuse. They are buying either a half an hour or an hour of your time. Paul or Cowboy will hand you a tag, white is for thirty minutes and pink is for an hour. You will then take them back to your assigned booth and then you are on your own. Paul or Cowboy will tell me or whoever is at the counter the customer's choice, that's how we'll keep individual counts. Don't never offer them anything. Let them tell you what they want. Questions?"

"What are the rates, Sandra?" Maria asked.

"They're on the board at the counter, twenty five for thirty minutes and fifty for an hour, you are free to negotiate tips. Our hours of operation, Monday through Saturday, noon to midnight are also posted and business cards, with our phone number, are on the counter. We'll encourage appointments in advance."

"What if there's a problem?"

"You call for security fast! There is a door behind the counter that opens into the back hall, we can access you quickly from either the lobby or the parlor. Remember, you have a madam and security screening up front and you ladies are professionals, I expect you know how to handle the most common problems. Before you leave, you change into your street clothes, never wear your uniforms when you're outside this building. Are there any other questions?"

No one spoke.

"Okay ladies, here's the most important thing you need to remember. See that trailer over there," Sandra pointed at the trailer, "I want you to think of it like Pandora's box. If you open that door, you will not like what happens next."

"What's going on Sandra?" Maria asked.

"There will be men in there, they are friends of ours. Do you all understand that language?" The women nodded. "If that freak shows his head around here, he's one dead son of a bitch."

******

Less than a mile down Rte 24 from the business sat Bogue Loop Road on the west side of the highway. A few hundred yards back the loop was a small dirt road that wound its way back into the forest. An innocuous road sign was marked Tulip Lane.

"Bitches! Whores! Sluts!" He shouted as he stomped around the inside of the cabin. "Did you think I wouldn't find you?" He continued bellowing. "Now you want to come here, to my home with your unclean bodies and your filthy business." He turned over a table and the empty beer bottles sitting on it crashed into a wall and broke. He fell to his knees and clasped his hands together, "Please, Lord, grant me the strength to rid our paradise of these sinners!" He looked up at the ceiling as tears ran down his face. "Yes, Lord, I know they must be cleansed first...yes I am listening to you." He bowed his head, the room was silent as his sobbing stopped. Minutes went by and he slowly raised his head. His thin lips spread into a psychotic smile. "Yes, Lord, time. You will send me a sign when it is time. Thank you, Lord."

******

"Sandra, can I talk to you privately for a minute?"

"Sure Maria." Sandra sat at the picnic table on the back deck as the sun started to go down. Maria was one of the older women and clearly one of the leaders within the group.

"I know you, you're Sandra Love. I know you were a call girl for the mob in Chicago and you worked undercover for the feds in Newport, Tennessee."

Sandra's green eyes narrowed. "That's a lot of knowledge, how did you come by that?" Sandra lit a cigarette as she stared at the young woman across from her.

"You killed a hit man and three other men, one named Norman Dixon."

Sandra put the cigarette up to her lips and inhaled, the smoke slowly ebbed out of her mouth as she held her stare. Her poker face never changed. Maria tapped her fingers on the picnic table, nervously.

"You're wondering how I know?" Maria's dark brown eyes darted from Sandra's gaze.

No response.

"Do you remember The L Sisters? Lola is my sister. Her real name is Anna Rose."

Sandra's face softened, "Damn girl, I thought I was going to have to take you out in the forest and leave you for dead. How's my Lola doing?"

"After Newport, she came to live with me and my husband in Jacksonville. I married a Marine too. When we split, she went back to Texas. She got married and has three kids. She thought a great deal of you, Sandra, she talked about you all the time. She hated that asshole she worked for...Dixie."

"Have you told her about me?"

"No, Sandra. That first night when you met with the girls and told us your name, I was pretty sure you were her. Then when you told us about your background and left out Newport, I wasn't sure, but then I realized you must be in the witness protection program or something. I knew it would be important not to tell anyone."

"That was smart, Maria. So why are you telling me now?"

"Two reasons. First, Anna told me she never had an opportunity to thank you. So I'm going to do that now. Thank you, Sandra."

Es nada, hermana.

Maria smiled at Sandra's Spanish. "And second, if I can help you like you helped Anna, please just ask me."

"You can do me two favors."

"What?" Maria put her elbows on the table and her head in her hands pulling her thick black hair back away from her face.

"Tell your sister I'm happy for her. Second, help me keep the girls away from the trailer, they're curious, they could blow this whole thing up."

"Feds inside?"

"Friends inside."

"Okay, I'll ride herd for you, Sandra."

"What do you think?" Farmer asked as he looked at the bank of monitors in front of him and the image of Sandra and Maria as they sat on the deck talking.

"It's an all or nothing situation, either he comes, we catch him and Hollywood makes a movie about us, or he doesn't come, we don't catch him and we have to ride out the next fifteen years of our careers with the tag, those idiots in the trailer." Strong said sarcastically.

"Hmmm... I wonder what my wife will wear on the red carpet?" Farmer mused.

"While you're figuring it out, did you figure out a schedule for us?"

"Yea, here, let me know if you want to change it." Mac reached behind him, his jacket hung off the back of the chair. He pulled a piece of paper out of his pocket and handed it to Strong. "Noon to midnight, six days a week. Six, six hour shifts apiece starting Monday. I'll take the second shift for the first week and we can alternate each week. Back up numbers are at the bottom."

Strong looked at the schedule, "Sounds good."

Mac looked at Sandra on the monitor that covered the back deck. "What's your take on her, Derrick?"

"That's the $64,000 question, isn't it? I've never met anyone like her in my life." He stepped in behind Mac and looked at the monitor as Sandra and Maria sat talking at the picnic table. "My father raised me not to judge people. The Bureau taught me how to judge people, she's a paradox for sure. Beautiful, earthy and smart as hell; good sense of humor, kind and giving, a real people person, but there's something different...something. I just can't put my finger on it."

"Exactly. Why the hell does she live in the woods so isolated from the world. She could be anything she wants to be. She's a one-eyed Jack alright." Mac stared at the monitor.

"Maybe the world let her down, maybe she's doing exactly what she wants to do. There aren't many of us that have that luxury in our lives." Strong commented.

"I wouldn't call that trailer of hers luxurious, Derrick."

"More like scary?"

"Yea, the trailer and her."

"What woman isn't? They all scare me, that's why I'm a bachelor."

Farmer laughed.

"Paul, Cowboy, will you guys come out here for a minute?" Sandra shouted into the house from the back door. In a few moments the two men appeared on the deck.

"What's up, Sandra?" Paul asked.

"What are the others doing?"

"They're changing and watching TV in the parlor."

"It's time you all met our friends." Sandra escorted the three over to the trailer and knocked four times on the door. Strong opened the door and they went into the trailer. "Paul, Cowboy, Maria, this is Special Agent Derrick Strong with the FBI and Special Agent Mac Farmer with the SBI."

After the introductions Sandra spoke, "It's important you all know each other by sight, don't want anyone down by friendly fire." Everyone agreed.

Then Derrick Strong spoke. "It is getting dark and we want you guys to see our setup. After this, treat this trailer as deserted. The only light we have in here is from the monitors and that space heater, with those black curtains over the windows it will look deserted. Come over here and we can show you the setup."

They all stood behind Mac as he showed them the monitors and recording devices including the zoom features on the cameras outside. "This is good when there's light," Mac explained, "but after dark, it's crucial that you turn on all the lights, especially the flood lights we had installed on the back of the building, otherwise we're blind."

"We have spares for all the lights behind the counter," Sandra told them. Paul and Cowboy nodded.

"Are you two carrying?" Strong asked.

Paul reached behind his back and pulled out a 9mm semi-automatic. Cowboy lifted his pant-leg up, the same weapon was holstered above his boot.

"Permits?" Strong asked.

Both men showed them their permit to carry a concealed weapon.

"Starting Monday, we'll be here in six hour shifts, changing at 6pm. We have the layout inside your building, if anything happens, you hear shots, you stay in the house, protect the women and call 911; we'll catch the bad guys. If we need to enter, we'll knock four times on the door, got it?"

"Got it," Paul responded.

"How about you big guy?"

"Got it," Cowboy followed.

"Nice meeting you all, good-bye."

"Thanks guys, good luck." Sandra said as they left the trailer.

As they walked back to the house Sandra "Are we ready for Monday?"

"I'd say we're ready for anything," Paul said.

"Nice job Sandra," the normally quiet Cowboy affirmed, "now I know why Momma Rabbit asked you to help."

"Do you think he'll come, Sandra?" Maria asked.

The four of them stepped up on the deck. Sandra turned and looked out at the ink black forest behind them. She stared into the dark, "He'll come."

The Storm of The Century

The business opened on Monday, January 19th. Around 4pm two men in their thirties opened the front door and walked up to the counter.

"Good afternoon, gentlemen, how can I help you?" Sandra asked. Paul sat in a chair behind the counter.

"We saw your sign and thought we'd stop in and check out your business," one of them said with a smile on his face.

"Well, thank you. We have several openings available this afternoon or would you care to make an appointment for another day?"

"We have time right now, how does it work?"

"We have two massage appointments to choose from, thirty minutes or an hour. Our rates are here on the board. You choose which one you'd prefer, then you meet with your masseuse in our parlor and she will take you back to her room where you can discuss what you want."

"What if we don't like our masseuse?"

"All of our massage therapists are professionals and we guarantee our work. We have six therapists working today, if for any reason you change your mind, just come back out and we will refund your money. Fair enough?"

The two men looked at each other, then the one who had spoken said, "Sure that sounds good. What would you recommend for our first visit?"

"Well, it depends on how long it's been since your last massage. If it's been more than a month, I'd go with the thirty minute massage, it's a good start. If you're use to getting massaged regularly, I'd recommend one hour. I'm sure you'll enjoy either." Sandra knew that most men this age wouldn't admit to not having been *massaged* for more than a month. The men took two one hour appointments. After they paid, and received their pink tags, Paul escorted them into the parlor. As the door opened and the men saw the six girls in their uniforms, Sandra heard one of them gasp, "Damn!"

Word spread quickly and by Saturday night a mix of locals and regulars from Jacksonville found their way to the new Evelyn's. The parlor had several men watching the new ESPN channel as they waited for their therapist. Paul and Cowboy were both on Saturday night, Paul up front and Cowboy in the parlor.

At the end of the night Sandra and Paul were at the front counter while Cowboy waited for the girls to change.

"How did we do this week, Sandra?"

"A little over two grand, not bad for the first week, it will get better."

"They seemed to like the uniforms and the parlor."

"Product differentiation, Paul, this business is all about presentation." She gave him a handful of money. "See that Cowboy gets his share, I'll see you on Monday."

Cowboy and the girls came out into the lobby. They all thanked Sandra as they swapped stories about the new business. Paul stepped outside into the light cast by the two pink bulbs on either side of the front door. After clearing the lot, he pulled the van up, Sandra turned off the outside lights, put the "closed" sign on the front door and locked up. They all got into their vehicles and left. A few minutes later Farmer locked the trailer door, got in his car and went home.

The next few weeks were routine. Business picked up and it seemed there were always two or three cars in the parking area. Sandra began making day trips up to Raleigh on Sundays and visiting Evelyn Monday morning on the way back. She introduced Jerry to the business and the cat quickly made his way from behind the counter to the parlor, but there was no sign of their man, nothing.

After six weeks of surveillance the two agents' patience was wearing thin. The temperatures on the coast had been unusually cold that week, controlled by a huge Canadian high stalled over the mid-west. Sandra spent Sunday, March 1st with Lane and family. Monday morning she headed back to the Crystal Coast as snow began to fall across the Triangle area. She arrived at the salon at noon. Cowboy, Maria and three other girls were waiting in the van. Farmer's car was in the lot. Sandra got out of her truck with Jerry in one hand and her overnight bag in the other, she opened the front door.

As the girls went back to change, Sandra and Cowboy talked. "I drove down from Raleigh this morning, we have some weather coming our way, snow, can you believe it, in March?"

"We get snow down here about every nine or ten years. It's pretty, but then the temps go up and it's gone in a day, usually no more than a couple of inches."

Sandra handed him twenty five dollars. "Run down to the Pig for me and pick up some bread, milk and cereal and some cold cuts; whatever the girls want to drink and some snacks, pretzels, chips, you know what I mean. If we get stuck here overnight, I want us to be prepared. Check on our coffee and pick up a pack of cigarettes for me."

"You going to be alright?"

"Farmer's in the trailer and we'll be fine in here," Sandra took off her new white Spyder ski jacket, her Colt .45 was in a holster across her hip.

"Back in awhile." Cowboy smiled as he turned toward the door and left.

As the day went by the snow started coming down and the wind picked up. A sudden shift in the low coming up the coast and the high moving in from the west created high winds in a corridor across North Carolina, but the shift happened so fast that there was no warning until early evening. Sandra was at the counter when the phone rang a little after 5pm.

"Evelyn's Massage and Day Spa, how can I help you?"

"Sandra, it's Derrick, what's your weather up there?"

"Last time I looked it was starting to snow."

"I'm in Jacksonville and we have almost a foot of snow, nothings moving."

"Have they started plowing yet?"

Derrick took the phone away from his ear and looked at it queerly. He put it back up to his ear. "Sandra, this isn't Chicago, there aren't any plows down here."

"I haven't looked outside recently, let me check." Sandra opened the front door, a few feet of snow had drifted against the front door, it collapsed into the lobby.

"Holy Shit!" Sandra gasped, "Cowboy!" She shouted at the top of her lungs.

Cowboy opened the parlor room door, his gun at the ready; the girls peered out from behind him.

"We have a problem, dude. Your couple of inches looks like a couple of feet, and that wind. Help me get this door closed. You guys, get out of your uniforms and put your street clothes back on, we're closed!" Sandra took the closed sign off the wall and placed it on the front door.

With one huge push Cowboy closed the front door and knocked half of the snow back outside. Sandra raced over to the phone. "Derrick, it's bad and it's drifting. The snow is coming down sideways and hard. The wind is gusting, I'd say about thirty to forty miles per hour."

"Turn on the news, Sandra, this thing came out of the blue and it's suppose to hit the coast the hardest. They're talking about snowfall in excess of two feet and winds up to sixty miles per hour."

"How long is it suppose to last?"

"They said the snow should stop by tomorrow night, but nothing is going to be moving before Wednesday or Thursday."

"What about the Marines, they have equipment that will more than handle—"

"What do you want me to do, Sandra, call the base and tell them that there are a half dozen people in a massage parlor in Bogue, could you send a couple of guys up in a Snow Trac? We're concerned because there's a maniac running around, but he hasn't shown up in six weeks!"

"Yes, damn it, and ask them if they could pick up a pack of cigarettes for me on the way."

Strong laughed out loud. "Girl, you are priceless. Do you guys have any food to eat?"

"Yes, I sent Cowboy out at noon, we should be okay. What about Mac?"

"If the snow is blowing as bad as you say it is, the camera lenses are probably going to get covered. When he can't see anymore, he'll come over, remember, four knocks."

"Got it."

"Are the lights on outside?"

"Yes."

"Okay, sit tight, only a moron would be out in this weather."

"A moron or a maniac," Sandra responded.

"Just be careful. You're on your own for a couple of days. Call if you have any problems. We're stuck here too."

"Will do." Sandra hung up as Cowboy finished sweeping up the snow and dumping it into a trash can.

"Cowboy, get the news on the TV, Farmer will probably be over soon."

The six of them sat in the parlor as Cowboy changed the channel from ESPN to the local news. Reporters and weathermen were trying to explain what had happened and why the storm was so under reported, no one had anticipated the quick and severe drop in temperatures as the two systems moved north and east. After watching the news for a half an hour, Sandra asked Cowboy to turn it off. She sat in one of the lounge chairs, Jerry on her lap.

"Listen up, ladies, if you watch that for too long, the drama will scare the hell out of you. No one is suppose to go anywhere except those young reporters, with the good hair, who are outside with a cameraman filming the storm."

The girls smiled.

"Eight years ago, I spent a winter in The Smokey Mountains, with a rifle, a backpack and Jerry." Jerry was licking Sandra's hand. "We literally lived in a cave, and we lived on what we could find to eat or kill."

"Sandra, are you bullshitting us?" Cowboy asked as he leaned forward in his chair.

"Cowboy, I swear on my mother's grave, what I'm telling you is true." Cowboy slowly sank back into the chair. "So, you can imagine that being here with food, water, power and your wonderful company, pales in comparison. Having said that, there are a few things we should talk about if we're going to be here for the next few days."

The wind outside started to blow harder and you could now hear it howling through the walls.

"You got our attention, Sandra." Maria assisted.

"We should have enough food to last three days, but we'll have to ration, no sneaking food." Cowboy looked chagrined. "We have cereal, sandwiches and snacks. Coffee, soda and water. We have a working TV, six beds and the sofa and you have me, Cowboy and—"

KNOCK! KNOCK...KNOCK! KNOCK!

Two of the girls screamed and jumped, frightened by the sudden knocking on the front door.

Sandra stood up and pulled her .45. Cowboy reached down and pulled his 9mm out. "Cowboy, open the door and stay behind it, it should be Mac. If it isn't, don't fire unless there's reason, could be a stranded motorist. I'll cover the door from this side. Ladies, don't move."

Cowboy moved to the front door, he looked over at Sandra, she stood with her gun pointed at the door. He unlocked it and then he pulled it open as he stepped back.

The wind howled and a blinding blast of snow blew into the lobby. A man launched himself into the room and fell on the floor covered in snow.

Sandra wheeled and pointed her gun at the
Cowboy closed the door with his back, his gun
pointed at the snow covered body.

"Mac is that you?" Sandra shouted. There was
so much snow on his body and head, she
couldn't tell if it was Farmer or not.

Aughhh... the man on the floor moaned, "I've
never been this cold before in my life." He rolled
over and through his snow covered eyes he saw
a pistol pointed at his face. "Jesus Sandra! Put
that thing away."

Sandra holstered her pistol, grabbed Farmer
and helped him up. As Cowboy put his gun
away, Sandra turned to him, "Be sure you lock
the door before you come in." She brushed
snow off of Farmer's head, "Come on, Frosty, I'll
buy you a cup of coffee." Sandra led Farmer into
the parlor. "Ladies, I want you to meet a friend of
ours, Special Agent Mac Farmer with The State
Bureau of Investigation."

The women stared as Farmer raised his hand in
acknowledgement and turned toward Sandra,
"Where's the coffee?"

The next few hours the storm grew. It was a
perfect storm. The seven sat in the parlor that
evening watching the news as report after report
came in to the station. The low coming up the
coast had initially thought to have been too far
off shore to have any significant effect, but as
the cold front swept east it suddenly veered
north and created a vacuum of upper air that

sucked the low into the corridor across North Carolina, then the two systems stalled. Reporters called it *bombing* and reported *thunder snow* across the region. Power had gone out in a number of communities and shelters had been set up in Jacksonville and Morehead City.

The group stayed up late and watched The Tonight Show with Johnny Carson, they turned in around 1am, Farmer on the sofa in the parlor and the rest in the back rooms. Tuesday morning Sandra woke up around 6:30am. She could hear the wind blowing hard outside the building. She visited the bathroom with her overnight bag, then she went out to the parlor. Mac sat on the sofa with a coffee and the TV on low. "Morning," he greeted her.

Sandra grabbed some coffee, lit a cigarette and sat down. "How bad?"

"Bad! They're calling it 'The Storm of the Century', nothing's moving. Hospitals and some of the towns are calling for volunteers with four wheel drive vehicles. I don't think too many folks are lining up. The only people outside on TV are reporters and Marines. The reporters are the ones with long hair."

"Has it stopped yet?"

"No, not until tonight. This is going to be a couple of feet of snow and the wind, look out the window, it looks like there are drifts across Rte 24 waist deep."

The Return of Sandra Love

Sandra went to the front window in the lobby, the snow had drifted up to the bottom of the window and it went straight across Rte 24 like a big white lake. "That's not beautiful, that's scary."

"I didn't think anything scared you," Mac replied.

"Why did you think that?"

"You have a real *tough girl* attitude toward life."

"Maybe my life's been a bit tougher than most."

"Is that why you live all alone in the forest?"

"Mac, up until a few months ago, I lived there with my husband. Before that, I lived in an apartment in Charlotte."

"Sandra, I've been a police officer all my life, I've worn four badges. I've been trained to read people, you're the biggest enigma I've ever met. Can't get a read, I suspect there's more than one person inside that head."

"Mac, I like you. You're a good guy, I've learned to tell the good ones from the bad. This isn't the way I planned to start the day, but I'll let you take a peek, if that's what you want?"

"Yes."

Sandra told him her back story as Mac sat on the couch intrigued. When she was done, he stood up and poured himself a second cup, he walked over to where she was seated, pot in hand. "It seems you've spent a great deal of your life hiding, either yourself or your background from people. I think I understand why you enjoy the forest. Thank you for sharing that with me, it will stay with me, and me only. More?"

Sandra held out her cup and Mac poured, "Your welcome. You seem like someone I can trust."

"I've got your back."

"I like that!"

"What do you like?" Cowboy asked as he walked into the parlor.

"Look out the front window," Sandra covered quickly.

Cowboy went to the window and looked out. "Damn! Never seen anything like this before."

Maria came out followed by Kim, Nicky and Jill, a red-head with long beautiful hair. "Is it still snowing?" Maria asked. She and the others went to the window and looked out. "Wow, it's beautiful," she said softly as the other three joined her looking at the storm.

Cowboy stood behind them, "And deep."

Tuesday, the snow continued falling and the wind howling. The seven watched television and played poker with a deck of cards Nicky had in her purse, she liked solitaire. Cowboy had purchased a huge bag of Fritos and another big bag of pretzels. Each player took ten corn chips and ten pretzels. The pretzels were worth two corn chips, they played for food.

The Fight in The Forest

Wednesday morning the forest was still. The beauty of the woods after the snow storm was majestic. Some of the smaller Carolina Pines were bent over to the ground weighted down with snow. All the trees were wearing their dress whites and the sun glistened off the white forest floor. Fox squirrels were running on top of the snow, as if they were playing tag. The temperature was in the high forties, headed for the high-fifties by afternoon. Sandra, Mac and Cowboy had boots and jackets for the weather, but the girls had brought light jackets and leather boots, unprepared for the conditions. They watched from the lobby as first Mac, then Cowboy and Sandra opened the front door and stepped down into the four foot high drift.

"I can't move in this," Sandra shouted as the girls watched her struggle, "Mac, I have a shovel in the back of the truck, can you get over there?"

"I'll get it!" Cowboy shouted as the taller and bigger man made his way through the drift. As he slowly high-stepped over to the parking area and Sandra's truck, he hollered back, "Check this out!" Cowboy had walked out of the drift and into a few inches of snow. He jumped up into the truck bed and rooted around until he found the shovel. He freed it and jumped down, making his way back to the drift. He started to shovel, the big man was like a machine, it took him about twenty minutes to clear a path through the drift and back to the front door.

"Sandra, I think we can get your truck out, but I didn't see any tracks on Rte 24. Until this melts off a bit, I don't think we're mobile, we could get stuck in a drift on the highway. Let's eat."

"Go get a sandwich, I just want to take a look around." Cowboy propped the shovel up in the snow and went inside. Mac and Sandra walked out to the parking area, the walking was easy. Sandra walked to the back of the building, "Check this out, Mac."

Farmer followed her over as Sandra pointed at the back deck, there was no snow on the deck! "Mother Nature, funny how she works, four feet in front, nothing in the back."

Farmer looked at the deck, "That's just weird."

By noon the snow was melting at a rapid rate. Temperatures were on the rise and news reports stated that Thursday's high would be in the sixties. As the group ate lunch, Maria asked, "Can we make a snowman? I've never made one before."

"I'll show you how," Cowboy offered.

"I guess it would be alright out front," Mac said, "I've got to clean off the lenses before tonight anyway."

The Fight in the Forest

"We'll all go together, I won't feel comfortable until I see some traffic on the Rte 24." Sandra said.

After lunch the group went outside. They walked the path Cowboy had shoveled and when they reached the parking area Cowboy started to roll the snowman in the front yard as Mac went around back to check on the lenses while Sandra watched from the front doorway.

WHUMP! The snowball hit Cowboy in the back of the head and knocked his hat off into the snow. He turned around and the four girls stood behind him with snowballs in their hands. The fight was on!

"Okay, someone is going to eat snow!" He bent over and grabbed some snow, then he charged. The girls threw their snowballs and ran laughing and screaming in different directions.

The phone rang at the counter and Sandra went inside to answer it. "Evelyn's Massage and Day Spa, how can I help you?"

"Sandra, it's Derrick—"

BAM! BAM! BAM!

The three shots came from outside. Sandra dropped the phone and drew her .45. She ran to the front door and looked out, no one was in sight. She stepped down onto the path and moved cautiously toward the parking area.

289

"HELP...PLEASE...SOMEONE... HELP...."

She recognized Nicky's voice and moved around the building until the trailer came into sight. Mac Farmer lay on his back in the snow in front of the trailer to her right. His body was still.

"PLEASE...SOMEONE... HELP! SANDRA... WHERE ARE YOU? HELP US..."

Sandra moved forward and saw Kim, Nicky and Jill kneeling on the ground around Cowboy. Sandra scoped the woods with her pistol, she couldn't see anything. She ran over to the four. Cowboy was shot in the right chest. "Kim, go in the house and grab some towels, fast!" The young black woman ran like the wind. "Nicky, when she gets back here, towels over the wound and pressure with both hands. Jill, go in the house and call 911, tell them what's going on and tell them to get someone here fast, now go!"

Sandra unzipped Cowboy's jacket and ripped his shirt open, a bullet wound was an inch above his nipple, blood trickled out and ran down his belly. Sandra reached down into the snow and grabbed several handfuls that she packed over the wound.

"Sandra..." Cowboy struggled.

"What happened, Cowboy?"

"He..."

"Slowly, Cowboy."

"...was behind the trailer. He...took out Mac...one shot...then he got me...he t-took Maria...I'm sorry...I'm sorry..."

"Son of a bitch! Where the hell is Kim?"

"Right behind you, Sandra."

Sandra took two towels, double folded them and placed them on the packed snow on Cowboy's chest. "Now, Nicky, right here." Nicky pressed down on the towels. "If you get tired have Kim or Jill spell you for awhile, but don't release the pressure until the ambulance gets here." Sandra turned to Kim, "Check Farmer out, I'm going after this bastard."

Kim grabbed Sandra's arm, "Sandra, this guy is big, bigger than Cowboy. He pistol whipped Maria and threw her over his shoulder like she was nothing. Please, stay here, Jill's calling the cops now."

"We don't even know if they can make it here, Kim, I have to go now, for Maria. Take this." She handed her Cowboy's gun. "You know how to use this?"

"Honey, I married a Marine too!" She released the gun's safety.

Sandra turned and followed the footprints in the snow. The forest was naked with snow; easy to see ahead. Sandra kept her eyes a hundred yards ahead of her as the footprints she followed dropped down a slope and south toward where she, Sara and Lane had hunted. The snow was less than two feet deep, in some areas only a few inches, and in other areas there were deep drifts. The prints led into the thickets, they were covered with snow and impossible to see through. A perfect place for a trap.

On the other side of the thickets, he waited behind a tree. Maria's body lay in the snow on the edge of the thickets. *Come on bitch,* he thought, *stick your head out of those thickets and I'll blow your brains out.* He waited. He knew it would be impossible for anyone to move through the snow covered brush without detection. The falling snow would announce her arrival like the snap of a mousetrap when the rodent goes for the cheese. He smiled as he pictured Sandra's death.

"Toss that gun into the thickets, or I will blow your head off."

The man froze. He didn't move.

"Take a good look around asshole, if you don't toss that gun this is the last thing you will ever see." He was absolutely motionless.

"You'll never hear three." The voice behind him was calm. "ONE...don't think, just toss it."

He still didn't move.

"TWO..."

He still didn't move.

The Fight in the Forest

"THR—"

He tossed the gun into the snow.

"Now turn around, and do it real slow."

The man turned around and faced Sandra. She looked at his contorted face, "Jamie?" Sandra gasped.

"Hello, bitch."

"Jamie Howell?"

"My name is Gabriel, whore."

Sandra stood there in shock. She looked at the face of the friend she had known for more than three years. "Why, Jamie, why?"

"I am the Lord's messenger, whore. Do not question the Lord."

Sandra's shock turned to anger, "Well, I got a message for you asshole, thou shall not kill. Now back up."

The big man took a few steps backwards. Sandra looked down at his feet, he was wearing Pastor John's galoshes. Sandra made her way over to Maria's body and knelt down. She had a deep cut on top of her head and was bleeding badly; she was unconscious and cold as ice. Sandra stood up. "We have two choices, you pick her up and carry her back or I shoot you in your knees and I carry her back, which will it be?" Jamie Howell's eyes seemed fixed and glazed, she wondered if he even heard her.

"The Lord has given me wings, I will fly her back."

"Good choice." Sandra motioned with her gun and Jamie lumbered over as Sandra backed up toward the thickets. He walked slowly toward Sandra, his eyes rolled up in his head as if in a trance. "That's far enough. Now pick her up." He turned his back to Sandra, reached down and picked Maria up. Then he turned swiftly around toward Sandra, his jacket was open and he held a Ka-Bar knife to Maria's throat.

"She must be cleansed first."

Shit! Sandra thought, *Think, Sandra think!*

He pressed the big knife against Maria's throat, her skin split and blood ran out of the wound.

"STOP! STOP, GABRIEL, STOP!"

He raised his head up and looked at Sandra.

"She's gone, Gabriel, feel her, she's cold as ice. The Lord has spoken to me. He said I must be cleansed before I can go to heaven, help me, Gabriel, help me!" Sandra fell to her knees.

"You must throw your weapon away, before you are cleansed." Sandra tossed her .45 over her shoulder it disappeared into the snow. Jamie dropped Maria and started toward her. She jumped up, turned around and looked for the impression in the snow where the gun landed. It was six feet away. She dove for the gun her bare hands digging in the snow! Suddenly, she was jerked up into the air! His gloved right hand covered her mouth as his left arm wrapped around her chest.

"Be not afraid, whore, I will cleanse thee and send you to our Lord." He turned and carried her back to where Maria lay, his Ka-Bar in the snow next to her. Sandra reached up with her right hand and grabbed his right thumb; her left hand dropped down and grabbed his left thumb, she pulled her two arms outward and his arms followed his thumbs. Sandra kicked her legs out from underneath her and she fell to her knees between his legs. She scrambled backwards and stood up behind him as he turned with fury in his eyes. He bent over and picked up the knife as Sandra backed away.

"You tricked me, you are a vile and evil whore!"

A police siren wailed in the distance, the sound echoed through the forest. Jamie turned his head.

"Hear the trumpets blowing, Gabriel? The end is nigh."

He rushed at her and thrust the big knife at her stomach, Sandra sidestepped backwards and to her right, the knife missed her by inches and she pushed him past her using his own weight against him. He turned and faced her.

"You will not escape the Lord!"

He charged again, she sidestepped again, this time to her left. He turned, he waved the knife back and forth in front of him. "When I am through with you, you will scream and beg the Lord for forgiveness."

Sandra stepped back and planted her right leg, she stood her ground, "Bring it on asshole."

He advanced toward Sandra, but this time more slowly. Suddenly, he thrust the knife forward directly at her face. Sandra's left arm came up and blocked his knife arm before the blade reached her, the knife passed over her head as she shifted her weight toward him and launched her booted right leg in a front snap kick, the toe of her boot crushed into his testicles!

AUGHHH... The big man dropped the knife and fell to his knees, both hands clutching his groin.

"That, you bastard, is for Zack!" Sandra turned her right hand into the shape of a *finger-gun.* She dropped her thumb down onto her middle finger and wrapped her forefinger around her thumb, the second knuckle on her forefinger stuck out like a miniature projectile. She stepped around him to his left, grabbed his hair with her left hand and pulled his head up. Then she drove her right knuckle into his left eye.

AIEEEEEE... His scream was high-pitched and inhuman. It filled the forest as loud as any of the military aircraft that flew over it periodically. He fell forward his left hand went up to his eye.

Sandra picked up the Ka-Bar, "And that's for Cooper."

"I'm blind...I'm blind...*AUGHHH...*"

"Remember this asshole, in the land of the blind, the one-eyed man is king!"

He lay in the snow in a fetal position moaning and sobbing.

Sandra placed her knee on his right side and the Ka-Bar against his throat, "And this is for me."

KAPOW!

The loud gunshot sounded like a cannon, it startled Sandra. She spun around and looked up the hill. Mac Farmer stood in the snow pointing his .357 mag at Sandra. "Don't do it, Sandra, he's sick."

"I took a vow, Mac. I gave my word to my boys..."

"I took a vow too, don't make me—"

"Go away, Mac, you won't cheat me out of—"

"Help pleeesss...S-Sandra...help meee..."

Sandra's head spun around, Maria was up on one arm, the other reached out entreatingly toward Sandra. Her face was covered in blood. "Mac, cuff this bastard!" Sandra ran to Maria.

Loose Ends and Best Friends

"What happened? I thought you were dead."

Mac tapped on his chest, "He's not the only one with a vest. The impact knocked me back, my head hit the trailer. I have no idea how long I was out, but when I woke up my head was in Kim's lap, she was rubbing snow on my face. It wasn't heaven, but close. Where did you study your martial arts?"

"Chicago, a man named Grayson, he worked for The Outfit, but he was a good guy."

The two followed the EMT's as they carried Maria up to the house on a stretcher. Behind them two deputy sheriff's from Bob Baker's office escorted a limping, handcuffed Jamie Howell, his left eye covered with bandages. When they got to the house the girls were out on the back deck and Sandra and Mac joined them as they watched the deputies escort Jamie out. Kim brought out a tray with a pot of coffee, packets of sugar and cups.

"You got him, Sandra, you saved Maria." Jill couldn't contain her excitement.

"No, Jill, and this is very important, Mac got him. I don't want to hear anyone say that I got him, do you understand?"

"But you did, Sandra," Nicky insisted.

"Mac took him down. This whole plan was Mac's and Derrick's, if I hear anything else, I'm going to have to tell Momma Rabbit that you've disappointed me. You understand that language?" The girls nodded. "Now, how's Cowboy?"

"He lost a lot of blood, but they said he'd be alright. They took him up to Carteret Hospital in Morehead City. They told us we did a great job, packing the snow on his chest. You saved his life too."

"No, you saved his life, understand."

Mac interrupted, "All of you, listen to me carefully. Sandra can't have her name or picture in the news, understand? If you screw this up, she could wind up dead. Now, thank her for saving your lives and let it go."

"You guys alright?" Mac and Sandra turned as Derrick Strong stepped up on the deck. "Nice work, buddy." He patted Farmer on the back.

"We'll talk later." Mac sipped his coffee as Sandra smiled.

******

The story hit the news Thursday and the papers Friday. The storm's story became yesterday's news fast as the DA held a press conference Friday morning announcing the capture of a suspect, and the arresting officers, Mac Farmer and Derrick Strong. The Crystal Coast was alive with talk about the case.

Friday afternoon Mac, Derrick, Sandra and a representative from the DA's office sat in Bob Baker's conference room at his office in Beaufort. The door to the conference room opened and Sheriff Baker walked in with another man dressed in an expensive suit, he was Asian. The sheriff introduced Dr. Haejin Chung, a prominent, forensic psychiatrist in North Carolina. "Dr. Chung has interviewed Mr. Howell and is prepared to provide us with his preliminary findings, Dr. Chung."

Chung removed the gold wire-rimmed glasses he was wearing and began cleaning them with a handkerchief he had pulled from his pants pocket. "First, let me start by telling you that it would be impossible for me to provide you with any certain diagnosis at this point. I can share with you what he related to me and I can tell you how he is presenting. In any case, Mr. Howell is a very sick man. As you may or may not know, he is a Vietnam veteran and as a corpsman he saw many terrible atrocities while serving there. He was also raised as a Christian and is well studied in the bible. He was married while he was in Vietnam and when he returned he discovered that his wife had been cheating on him. All of these issues drove him into a deep depression. He felt that his career would be threatened by his employer's discovery of his condition. Instead of seeking help, he sought hiding, and that led to his DID."

"DID?" Sandra asked.

"Dissociative Identity Disorder, he has all the signs. You may have heard it referred to as a multiple or split personality."

"You mean like Norman Bates in the Psycho movie?" Sandra asked.

"That is exactly what I mean."

"Can you explain what you mean when you say dissociative?" Bob Baker asked.

"It's the same as when you day dream, only much more severe. Based on our research, we think that it stems from trauma, in his case Vietnam and his wife's infidelity. Between the horror, the pain, and the fear of discovery he used the disassociation to handle his depression. He sought solace in the good book, he found it there, in Gabriel."

"Why was he after me? Why did he kill my dogs? Do you know if he drugged my punch at the VFW party?"

"Yes. He does a lot of volunteer work, he was a volunteer bartender that night. He said you danced very provocatively, he was attracted to you. You got up suddenly and left, on the way out you asked him for a glass of water, he slipped the drug into the water, not your punch.

He told me that he saw you helping the police in the forest, he considered you and your husband friends, he saw that as a betrayal, similar to his wife's. The dogs were a warning, but he also admits to trying to kill you at your home after he saw you with a woman who ran a brothel in Jacksonville; he tried to kill her with his car."

"With shells he stole from the base." Strong commented.

"Yes, he told me they were armor piercing, Gabriel liked them. He also has a vest and some anesthetics he stole from the hospital. He lives on Tulip Lane, off Bogue Loop Road, you'll find everything there including his car."

"I'd like to ask a question Dr. Chung, my name is George Albert and I work in the district attorney's office. If he's in the Jamie Howell persona, how does he remember what Gabriel likes?"

"Excellent question. There are some cases of DID that involve amnesia, but they are more infrequent. It is more common that the patient is aware of the other persona, like the Jekyll and Hyde story, they can remember the switching process, but they can't control it. The patient feels more like a passenger, than a driver."

"Isn't there a lot of controversy in the mental health field about DID and whether it really exists?"

"No, but you're close. The controversy is centered around legal cases where the defense claims DID when it actually does not exist with the individual charged. There are some mental health professionals who believe that it is very rare and when diagnosed is often accompanied by a companion diagnosis, as in Mr. Howell's case, schizophrenia."

"You're also saying he's schizophrenic?"

"Mr. Albert, God talks to Mr. Howell. I really don't think the district attorney has to worry about an insanity plea, in my opinion he is not currently able to defend himself in court."

"Thank you, Dr. Chung. That's really all I need to know." Mr. Albert thanked each person for their assistance and excused himself.

Sheriff Baker shook his head, "Now that we have an all volunteer military, I hope we'll see them getting better treatment than our Vietnam vets received."

"War is hell, Bob," Mac commented, "those who pay no attention to history, are doomed to repeat it."

Bob Baker stood up, "Mac, Derrick, thank you." They shook hands. He turned to Sandra, "I want to offer you a job, but you already have one, don't you? Take whatever time you need, there will be no hassle from my office." He extended his hand to Sandra. "I told you the first time we met in the forest, I thought we'd wind up friends."

******

"Well, I guess this is goodbye," Sandra said. The three of them stood outside the courthouse.

"You've got my card," Farmer said, "anything, anytime." He extended his hand.

"You're kidding right? This is the south, Agent Farmer." She hugged him and he smiled. She turned to Derrick, "You too, Agent Strong."

The two embraced, "It was a real pleasure, Sandra." Derrick told her.

"Me too." Sandra raised her right hand and squeezed it into a fist, "Be strong!"

The two men watched her as she walked away, got into her truck and left. Sandra drove down to the Carteret Hospital in Morehead City, her first stop was Maria's room.

"How you feeling today? I brought a friend with me."

Maria's head was wrapped in bandages. She turned her head slowly and looked over at Sandra, she stood at the entrance to the room holding Jerry Crosby Miller.

"Hi, Sandra. Oh, Jerry, can I pet him?" Sandra put Jerry down on Maria's lap. He nestled in and started purring as she stroked his head.

"How's your head?" Sandra asked.

"They were worried about my brain bleeding, but they took pictures of it and the doctor said I will be fine. They had me up and walking around this morning. I'm going home Monday and I have a surprise for you."

"The bill?"

Maria smiled. "Anna is flying up tonight, she's going to be in town for a week, she wants to see you."

"My Lola? That's great! I want to see her too. I'll be back tomorrow."

Sandra visited for a while and then left to see Cowboy. When she walked in Paul was standing next to his bed and Evelyn was in a wheelchair her back to the door. The big man was sitting up, a pizza box sat on his lap.

"Well, looky here," Cowboy said, "I'm getting some loving tonight."

"How you feeling, big guy?"

"Get over here and I'll show you."

Sandra walked over to the side of the bed and Cowboy wrapped one arm around her neck and gave her a big kiss on the cheek. "Thanks, Sandra, I won't forget. You understand that language don't you?"

"You bet."

"How are you doing, Evey?"

"I'm rehabbing, come here."

Loose Ends and Best Friends

Sandra turned and knelt in front of the wheelchair. Evelyn leaned forward and gave her friend a hug, "Thanks, Sandra, I owe you one."

Sandra took Evelyn's hand and kissed it. She looked into her friend's eyes and whispered, *Alla famiglia.*

 Paul and Cowboy watched quietly. After the exchange was over, Sandra shared what Bob Baker had told her about the business. Evelyn told Sandra that the three of them would talk about the future of the business. They spent some time together, Sandra discussed how she wanted the press handled, should any of them be approached. They all agreed. Sandra gave Evelyn the key to the Spa's front door and left. She picked up Jerry in Maria's room before she drove home. When she arrived at her lot a van was parked on the side of the dirt road. A young woman jumped out with a microphone in her hand and a trailing cameraman.

"Miss Horne, I'm Mary Jones, would you mind if I ask you a few questions about Jamie Howell and how you caught him?" The cameraman pointed the camera at Sandra and the little red light came on. Sandra grabbed the young woman's arm and spun her around so their backs were to the camera.

"Kill the camera!" Sandra growled at the young reporter.

"Turn it off, Joe." The cameraman lowered the recorder.

"You seem like a nice person, Mary, do you do ambush interviews often?"

"Miss Horne, I'm just trying to do my job."

"If it's worth doing, it's worth doing well, wouldn't you agree?"

"Of course."

"Do you have a notepad?"

"Yes." She handed the mike to her cameraman and took a notebook out of her pocket.

"Mary, you can ask me any question you want and I will give you an honest answer, I just want three things agreed to, then the exclusive is yours, agreed?"

The reporter lowered her pad. "What are the three things?"

"I value my privacy, that's why I live where I live. No pictures, no description and no reference to where I live."

"Can I say, you live in the Croatan?"

"You may." Sandra lit a cigarette as the young reporter interviewed her asking question after question. Sandra kept to the story agreed to by all the parties. It never aired. As the two got into the van and left, Sandra let Jerry out of the truck and he followed her back to the trailer. As they walked into her front yard, she turned and picked up Jerry. She looked out at her beloved forest, "It's good to be home."

The Return of Sandra Love

Epilogue

Saturday morning, the phone rang in the kitchen, Lane picked it up. "Hello."

"Hello yourself."

"Hi, hon, how are you doing? We read about them catching the killer, pretty good work, eh?"

"Yes, reassuring isn't it. What are you doing for dinner?"

"Let me check with Jenny." Lane asked Jenny what she planned for dinner.

"Is that Sandra?"

"Yes."

Jenny held her hand out. Lane gave her the phone, "Find out what time she's coming." Lane walked over to the family room where Sara was watching TV. "Sandra's coming up today."

Sara jumped up from the couch, "When?"

"Nana is talking to her now, go get ready, we'll pick them up today."

"Hi, Sandra, it's Jenny. How have you been, hon?"

"Busy as hell, I'm ready for a vacation, can you put me up for a stay?"

"Your timing is impeccable, Sara is off next week for spring break, I'm pretty sure Lane's cleared his calendar. What time will you be here?"

"How's 5pm sound?"

"I was planning filets on the grille, or would you rather go out?"

"God no! I don't want to share you guys with anyone."

"Okay, see you at 5pm. Bye now." Jenny hung up the phone then she hung her head down. Lane came into the kitchen.

"Mom, you alright, what's wrong?"

Jenny grabbed a paper towel and dabbed her eyes, "I missed her, Lane."

"Mom." Lane walked over and hugged his mother-in-law. "What time is she arriving?"

"She said 5pm."

"Well, get yourself ready, we're going to pick them up this morning."

******

Sandra packed her suitcase and drove up to the hospital. She met her old friend from Tennessee and the three women spent the morning and afternoon together talking and reminiscing. She left for Raleigh a bit after 2pm. She pulled into Lane's at 5pm.

"Sandra's here!" Sara shouted as she ran back into the kitchen.

"Leave them in the box for now," Lane told his daughter as the three went to greet Sandra and Jerry at the front door.

"I really missed you all this week," Sandra said as she put down her bag and Jerry ran into the house.

As the four stood in the foyer, a whining sound came from the kitchen. "What's that?" Sandra asked.

"What's what?" Lane responded.

"I thought I heard..." Sandra paused, "...there it is again."

The three looked at each other. "I don't hear anything. Do you, Daddy?"

Sandra looked at their smiling faces. It's coming from—"

YIP...YIP...

"What have you done?" She looked at Lane.

"My client enters a plea of not guilty, your honor."

"We'll see about that, counselor." Sandra walked back to the kitchen as the others followed. In a brown cardboard box on the floor of the kitchen next to the island were two twelve week old Labrador Retriever puppies, one yellow and the

317

other chocolate. Sandra froze in her tracks and her hands went up to her face. "Oh, they're so cute! She bent over and picked up both of them. The chocolate snuggled between her breasts as the yellow licked her face. "What are their names?"

"We were going to wait for their mother to name them," Lane replied. "They're yours, Sandra."

"Oh Lane," she hugged the two puppies tightly.

"What are you going to call them, Sandra?" Sara asked.

"Oh gosh, Sara, I don't..." Sandra's eyes glanced around the room as she struggled for an answer. A box of candy sat on the far counter. Sandra grinned.

"How's Mike and Ike sound?"

About The Author

Steve Peters was born and raised in suburban
Philadelphia. He is a graduate of Penn State
University and a Vietnam veteran. After forty
years in Human Resources and Hospital
Administration, Steve and his wife Judy moved
to North Carolina to be close to their grand
children and North Carolina's beautiful Crystal
Coast.

Steve is a member of the Carteret Writers group.
He enjoys hunting, fishing, bridge, golf and
writing. Steve and his wife Judy live in Cape
Carteret, NC with their two Labrador Retrievers
Zach and Stu.

Other books by Steve Peters
The Outlaw Sandra Love
Something Dangerous

CPSIA information can be obtained
at www.ICGtesting.com
Printed in the USA
FFOW02n2140240217
32844FF